Penalty Shootout

Also by Bill Knox

PENALTY SHOOTOUT

Bill Knox

Constable • London

Constable & Robinson Ltd
3 The Lanchesters
162 Fulham Palace Road
London W6 9ER
www.constablerobinson.com

First published in Great Britain 1973 as *Draw Batons!*
This edition published in Great Britain by Constable,
an imprint of Constable & Robinson Ltd 2007

A copy of the British Library Cataloguing in Publication
Data is available from the British Library.

ISBN: 978-1-84529-638-4

Printed and bound in the EU

Chapter One

Police Sergeant Francey Lang looked down the deserted but brightly lit length of King Street Public Hall, approved the way gay banners and poster-covered display stands hid grimy walls and a cracked ceiling, and told himself he'd done a good job.

It was almost midnight and even the hall caretaker had given up, retiring to his cubby-hole of an office to brew another pot of tea. But tomorrow at ten a.m. the Project Community exhibition would come to life, Francey Lang's idea from the beginning, his first major accomplishment as community relations officer for Glasgow's Millside Division.

A tall, thin man with a raw-boned face slightly marred by an old razor-slash, he had been a beat cop for fifteen years before this new job had come his way. Wandering down the length of the hall, glancing at the display stands as he passed, he decided the change had been a good one. Community relations officers were new animals in every Scottish police force. A government-inspired innovation, they were shaping to be more useful than most of the notions that came from that direction. Community relations came down to a mixture of grass-roots crime prevention, social welfare and spreading the word that cops were people like everyone else. Francey Lang certainly reckoned the last part was overdue.

A busy squeaking from a road safety stand stopped

him briefly. Rustling around inside their cage, a cluster of trained white mice should delight the children being brought along from the local primary schools. The mice demonstrated road sense in a mock layout of street crossings – and the kids needn't know that one paw on the wrong area brought a tingle from concealed electric wiring.

Lighting a cigarette, Francey Lang continued his inspection past a crime prevention display, then down through a group of stands where the women's clubs of Millside would be represented. But he slowed appreciatively as he neared the model engineering section.

The hobby clubs had really gone to town. Model aircraft hung suspended over exact-scale ship miniatures. Tiny kit-built cars, an old-fashioned working steam engine in glinting brass and a chance to play noughts and crosses against an electronic machine built by the local technical college were all going to attract attention.

But his own favourite remained a long, trestle-mounted sweep of model railway track. Francey Lang stopped beside it, pushed the police cap back a fraction on his forehead, and knew a sudden nostalgia. Twin lines of narrow, glinting rail snaked their way through carefully painted scenery. They passed neat stations and matching signal boxes, dived into tunnels through humps of papier mâché mountain and weaved an intricacy of criss-cross junctions.

The control panel for it all was beside him. Idly, he flicked a switch and blinked in mild surprise as a red 'active' light glowed in answer.

Sergeant Francey Lang knew temptation – and the hall was empty. He touched the nearest control lever and a little blue shunting engine quivered against a set of buffers. Closing the lever, he stubbed his cigarette, looked back to make sure the caretaker wasn't around, then tried the next lever. A green locomotive and its string of Pullman coaches murmured to life and began to gather speed as he opened the lever wider. Clicking and clattering over a set of points, swaying as it took a curve, the train bustled past a station and vanished into a dark hole of a tunnel which sat like a rabbit burrow in the base of a large, carefully painted green hill.

A moment later there was a thud, a brief, frantic spinning of wheels and a drawn-out clatter. One of the Pullman coaches appeared, rolling over and over across the floorboards to halt near a litter bin.

Cursing, Francey Lang slapped the main switch off again. Model train enthusiasts didn't take kindly to people mucking about with their property and if anything was damaged there would be hell to pay. Hurrying over, he crawled under the poster-decorated trestles to reach the blind side of the dummy hill, scrambled upright – then froze where he was.

Still seated on a stool, a dead man lay slumped forward across the model track. A long, thin-bladed screwdriver protruded between his shoulders, his bald head lay against the inner shell of the papier mâché, and the wrecked Pullman train lay piled around.

One small corner of Francey Lang's mind struggled to remain operating. The dead man, middle-aged and with a face that was vaguely familiar, was in shirt-sleeves and had an expensive gold watch on his left wrist.

The way he lay across the track, it was a minor miracle the current had still managed to complete a circuit . . . not that it mattered. A low groan came from Francey Lang's lips and he closed his eyes in despair.

In ten hours' time the Chief Constable of Glasgow

was scheduled to perform the official opening ceremony for Project Community. Half of the police committee were coming, with a sherry and sandwiches reception organized in a side room. Opening-day invitations had been sent out to all the news media in the city – and on the promise that she'd meet the Chief Constable for sure, Lang's wife had bought a new dress.

Reluctantly, he opened his eyes again. The dead man was still there, the face remained hauntingly familiar.

Wearily, Francey Lang turned on his heel and trudged back towards the telephone in the caretaker's office.

Project Community – he'd only himself to blame.

The first C.I.D. car arrived three minutes later, abandoning a routine prowl along the High Street. Two more cars from the Divisional Office reinforced them moments later and from then on the pattern slipped into routine.

'Except we don't usually have to start with a cop playing at trains,' murmured Detective Chief Inspector Colin Thane. He sighed, glancing round the hall. 'Sergeant, explaining that part is going to be a problem.'

'Yes, sir.' Francey Lang flushed and swallowed hard. For the last half-hour, under orders to keep his nose out of everything, he'd been left stranded in a corner beside the white mice. 'I'm sorry, sir.'

'Still, it could have been worse.' Thane considered him sombrely.

'Sir?' Francey Lang found that hard to believe.

'Uh-huh.' Thane grinned a little. 'It might have been the Chief Constable who found him.'

He turned, leaving Lang to consider that possibility,

and walked down the hall towards the activity around the model railway.

'Hold it a moment, Chief Inspector,' hailed a voice.

He stopped obediently while a Scientific Bureau photographer, balanced precariously on a nearby counter, triggered his camera for a general view of the railway layout.

'Thanks.' The man scrambled down again and went off.

'He should have taken one of you while he was at it,' grumbled a familiar voice. 'Divisional chief arrives – late as usual.'

'It's called confidence in the system.' Thane turned and grinned at the small, grey, shabbily dressed figure who'd appeared beside him. Detective Inspector Phil Moss needed a shave and a clean shirt. But there was nothing unusual about that. 'How long since you got here?'

Moss grunted expressively. 'I was halfway out of the office, all set for home, when they caught me. You?'

'Newly in bed.' For once, Thane had planned an early night. Sleep had been in short supply around Millside Division during the past week, thanks to a wave of robberies and a couple of razor gang battles. 'I've talked to Francey Lang. What's the rest of it?'

'Not much. The caretaker saw nothing, heard nothing and knows even less.' Moss stopped and gave a jaundiced glare as another Scientific Bureau man, laden with equipment, collided with him. 'Damn it, can't you characters look where you're going?'

'Sorry.' The Bureau man strode on, blandly unconcerned.

'Give some people a magnifying glass and they think they rule the world.' Scowling, Moss watched the Bureau man bore on towards his destination, then turned back to Thane. 'Still, at least we've got a name for our body. In fact, you'll know him. It's Harry Durman, the car dealer.'

'Durman?' Thane raised a surprised eyebrow. 'What was he doing here?'

'Playing at trains, like Francey Lang. Or, at a guess from the tools lying around, doing a repair job on the track.' Moss took the cigarette Thane offered and shared a light with him. 'Anyway, I've sent Beech out to check his home. I don't think there are any relatives, but I thought we'd make sure.'

'Let's take a look at him,' said Thane wryly. 'Might as well get it over with.'

They walked together down the hall, the other police around easing back to let Thane through. Most were men from his own division, but all knew him by sight . . . even outsiders found Millside's C.I.D. chief easy to remember.

In his early forties, Colin Thane had close-clipped dark hair and a face even those in a friendly mood classed as cheerfully rugged. Wearing a soft brown lovat tweed suit, he filled its tailored lines in a burly, muscular fashion and moved with the controlled, athletic ease of a man still close to peak condition – though he carried more poundage than when he'd been a moderately successful amateur heavyweight with the police boxing team.

He was young to have a Division command. And Millside, a slice of the city which held everything from dockside slums onward, was as tough a division as any in Glasgow. But that was part of the reason he'd been given the job.

'Through here.' Moss gestured to a gap made in the trestle-supported track.

On the other side, Harry Durman still lay as he'd been found. The area around him was dusted grey with fingerprint powder, but the screwdriver had been removed from his back. Nearby, a figure in a blue pin-stripe suit was repacking a medical bag.

"Morning, Doc,' greeted Thane easily. 'Any luck?'

'Luck isn't what I get paid for.' Doc Williams, the city's senior police surgeon, glanced pointedly at his watch. 'Did you walk all the way?'

'I've been through that part already.' Grimacing, Thane joined him and looked down at the body. 'What can you say so far?'

The police surgeon shrugged. 'That you should wait for the full autopsy report.'

'Uh-huh.' Thane nodded mildly. Doc Williams could be temperamental on occasion, particularly in the middle of the night. 'But even a little would help.'

Williams sighed theatrically, then obliged.

'It looks like a single stab wound, angled downward, and plenty of force behind it. Penetration was slightly to the left of the vertebral column, just above the seventh interspace. That would take it directly into the heart, allowing for the angle. Death would be pretty well instantaneous.'

'Got the weapon handy?'

Wordlessly, Doc Williams held up a plastic bag which had already been tagged and labelled. Inside, the screwdriver had a thick, insulated rubber handle. Still stained with blood, the long blade was as slim as a knitting needle and ended in a narrow, finely shaped edge.

'No fingerprints,' contributed Moss at his elbow. 'The thing probably came from Durman's tool-kit.'

A canvas tool-roll lay open on the trestled planking beside the body. One of the empty spaces was a matching size and shape.

'Some people will borrow anything.' Doc Williams stifled a yawn. 'Still, a nice clean puncture wound makes a change from the usual mad axeman stuff you

11

turn up.' He laid down the screwdriver, then snapped his medical bag shut. 'Well, who'd want to murder a hobby-minded car dealer?'

'Almost anyone who bought second-hand from this one.' Thane answered absently, mentally assembling his priorities. 'Durman's idea of "fully reconditioned" was a fast one-coat respray. How about time of death, Doc?'

'Too recent.' Slowly, the police surgeon shook his head. 'On body temperature, about an hour with a give or take margin.' He glanced at Moss. 'Does that fit?'

'It might,' nodded Moss. 'The caretaker thought everybody left around eleven – people were wandering in and out till then, and the side doors were open.' Moss paused and scraped a long fingernail over his stubbled chin. 'Talking of doors being open, do we let this show go ahead?'

'No.' Thane pursed his lips, thinking of what that meant. 'I'll take care of that side.'

'Leave it till later,' murmured Doc Williams. 'There's an old saying, let sleeping Chief Constables stay that way. And talking of sleep' – reaching over, he picked up his medical bag – 'there's nothing more for me here. I'll have our friend on the autopsy table after breakfast and get the preliminary report to you before noon. There shouldn't be anything dramatic involved.'

Thane nodded, watched him stride off, then turned back to Moss. 'Where's the caretaker?'

'In his office, waiting. And I've got the secretary of the model rail club on his way over.'

Thane stayed silent for a moment, thinking how much they did know about Harry Durman. The used-car trade hadn't been his only activity. More than once his name had cropped up on the fringe of Millside cases, twice he'd almost been nailed for suspected fraud. But the most recent had been the most spectacular – when fire gutted a bingo hall in which he'd been half-owner. The fire had been late at night and afterwards the Headquarters arson squad had prodded around the ashes of the bingo hall without being able to prove anything. Finally, reluctantly, the insurance company had paid up.

But another man had been involved in the bingo hall affair, Durman's partner. Thane searched his mind for the name.

'Jarrold Walsh.' He said it aloud, saw Moss blink, and explained. 'Walsh, the gambling club king. He was Durman's partner on that bingo hall deal.'

'So?' Moss still looked blank.

'No real reason.' The fire had been back in January, it was now early May. And Jarrold Walsh ran one of the most profitable gambling clubs in town, an operation backed by interests in a scatter of other bingo halls. 'Phil, tell Records I want details of every known associate listed for Durman.'

Moss nodded, then gave a sudden grimace, followed by a monumental belch. Passing by, two plainclothes men glanced over with mild, unsurprised interest. Guarded against the medical profession in general and surgery in particular for almost ten years by its owner, Phil Moss's stomach ulcer was famed throughout the city's divisions. It was no ordinary ulcer, claimed his juniors. It was the day-to-day barometer of his outlook on life as second-in-command at Millside.

'When did you eat last?' asked Thane from experience.

'On schedule. But it was in the canteen – grease with everything.' Moss shuddered at the reminder, then abruptly changed the subject. 'Ready for the caretaker now?'

Before Thane could answer, a uniformed constable

came heading towards them at a trot from the far end of the hall. Reaching them, the man saluted Thane.

'Sir, we've had a radio call through Control for you. Detective Constable Beech at Durman's home – he says it is empty but he'd appreciate someone joining him.'

'To hold his hand?' asked Moss innocently.

Thane silenced him. 'Did Beech say why, Constable?'

The man nodded. 'There's been a break-in at the place, sir.' He grinned a fraction and relaxed a little. 'I – uh – well, he said he didn't know what the hell to do about it.'

Thane's own smile had faded. D.C. Beech wasn't the type who usually admitted he had problems. Dropping what was left of his cigarette on the floor, he stubbed it underfoot.

'Phil, I'll go. Take over again here – and, above all, try to find exactly what this caretaker was doing. Including why he didn't have some kind of control on the doors.'

Moss grunted an acknowledgement. 'And you'll come back here?'

'Soon as I can. This shouldn't take long.'

Thane started towards the main exit. Phil Moss stubbed his own cigarette, then spun on his heel and headed for the caretaker's office.

Harry Durman's apartment home was on the ground floor of a red sandstone tenement building in Fraser Street, on the west side of Millside Division. Fraser Street was respectable, middle-class, had flower boxes on most of its windows, and was mainly occupied by families who lived quiet, ordinary lives and went to church on Sundays. Crime usually meant some rampaging small boy had broken a window.

The Millside duty car reached there in an easy ten minutes, travelling along routes almost deserted of traffic and through streets where only a few lights here and there showed some people still hadn't gone to bed for the night. At Fraser Street it was the same, with one difference. Tightly parked lines of cars lay along both kerbs, locked and empty while their owners slept.

'It's No. 62.' Thane saw the driver frown at the parking problem as they crawled the last distance, checking house numbers. 'Just drop me off here and squeeze in somewhere further along – but keep listening to that radio.'

The man nodded, stopped the car, waited till Thane had climbed out, then slid it into gear again. As the red rear lights disappeared down the street, Thane stood at the kerb for a moment and shivered slightly in the cold night air while he glanced around.

Lit by a soft glow of street lamps, nothing else moving along its length, Fraser Street presented its usual peaceful face to the world. Not so much as a dog barked. But a chink of light showed as the ground floor curtains at No. 62 were twitched long enough for someone to look out.

Going in through a tiled entry, Thane found Durman's name on the left-hand door. Before he could reach for the bell-push the door swung open.

'I saw the car, sir.' Detective Constable Michael Beech, young, still fresh-faced, looked under-age to be a cop. In fact, he'd recently become the father of twins. Opening the door wider, he added, 'I didn't expect you to turn out on this.'

'It sounded interesting.' Thane came in and waited while Beech closed the door. 'Well, what's the story?'

'D.I. Moss sent me out here with Durman's keys, sir. The house door was locked but once I got in, well'

15

– Beech gestured across the tiny hallway towards a back room – 'see for yourself.'

Going over, Thane stopped in the open doorway, found the light switch, then whistled softly as a neon-tube light came to life. The room, a blend of study and workshop, had its cupboards and drawers lying open and their contents scattered. Though even without that it was an unusual room, littered with completed and partly assembled models and the raw materials for more.

'The window was forced, sir,' said Beech quietly. 'The other rooms got the same treatment as this – someone really turned the place over.'

'I'm beginning to be glad I came,' murmured Thane.

Beech at his heels, he checked the rest of the modestly furnished apartment. Every room showed it had been subjected to the same swift but thorough search. Returning to the back room, Thane went over to the window. It had a wooden frame and the snib had been forced, leaving deep jemmy marks. The paved back yard was about four feet below.

'Have you checked outside?' he asked.

Beech nodded. 'Before I radioed in, sir. I couldn't see anything. Then I went along to where I left my car, called Control – and afterwards came straight back here.'

'How about the neighbours?'

'I haven't talked to any yet, sir.'

Thane shrugged. Fraser Street was the kind of place where neighbours would certainly react if they heard anything.

Turning from the window, he looked around the room again. It represented the other side of Harry Durman's life, one of small-scale motors and intricate detail. Racks of tools ran along one wall, a neat miniature lathe was mounted on a bench top and hobby and technical journals were stacked in corners.

'Really went in for it, didn't he?' Beech thumbed almost enviously towards a sleek, silver-painted model aircraft suspended from the ceiling by an almost invisible wire. 'A 2.5 c.c. diesel engine and radio controlled in flight – they cost money.' He grinned. 'I used to read about them when I was a kid, but that was the nearest I got to owning one.'

For Thane it had been those majestic model yachts which glided across the local boating pond under full sail while he made do with a home-made hulk. Lips pursed, he wondered how much in hard cash Durman's hobby interests had cost him. And where the money had come from.

He beckoned Beech to follow and left to have a second tour of the apartment.

They were in the hallway when the doorbell rang. While the noise was still dying, a key grated into the lock.

Signalling Beech into cover, Thane pressed himself back behind the door as it swung open. A young man with dark, almost shoulder-length hair and a wisp of beard stepped confidently into the apartment with a large, paper-wrapped package in his arms.

'Harry – are you in?' he hailed cheerfully.

Without waiting for an answer he heeled the door shut behind him. Then he saw Thane for the first time and his mouth fell open. Recovering fast, he swallowed and frowned suspiciously.

'Who the hell are you?'

'That's what I was going to ask,' said Thane neutrally while Beech emerged from the bedroom. 'Do you live here?'

'No.' The youngster, who looked about twenty and wore a hip-length leather jacket over flared slacks and a knitted wool sweater, considered them carefully and reached his own conclusion. 'Police?'

'That's right.' Thane quietly showed his warrant card. 'Who gave you the key to this apartment?'

'Harry did – Harry Durman.' The new arrival glanced around, frowning, the package still in his arms. 'What's going on, anyway? Where is he?'

'He's dead,' Thane told him bluntly, watching for reaction.

'Dead?' The bearded mouth shaped a silent gasp. 'But – I mean how, what happened?'

Thane shrugged. 'Mind telling me what you're doing here first?'

'I – my name's Roy Davidson.' The youngster took a couple of steps towards the back room, then stopped as Beech eased across to bar his way. 'I'm a friend, more or less.' He nodded at the package in his arms. 'I promised Harry I'd bring this round to him tonight. He said he might be pretty late back, so he gave me a key.'

'And you use it after one a.m.?' Thane's face stayed wooden.

'Well, he wanted this thing badly.' Davidson looked around for somewhere to lay the package.

Beech took it from him and hefted it, glancing at Thane.

'Open it,' said Thane shortly.

'Hey' – anger flushed on Davidson's cheeks as Beech set to work – 'who said you could do that?' The wisping beard twitched at the way he was ignored and he swung on Thane. 'Look, I've already asked you. What happened to Harry? Was it some kind of accident?'

'He was murdered, Mr Davidson.' Thane paused, but the younger man just stared at him in a crushed silence. 'That's why we're here and why you interest me. How old are you?'

18

'Twenty.' Davidson swallowed hard. 'I'm a – a student. Second year at university, taking a science degree.'

Beech removed the last of the wrappings. Underneath was an oblong metal box holding a double line of dials and switches.

'Yours?' asked Thane.

'No.' Davidson bit his lip. 'It – well, I had it on loan, but it belonged to Harry and he wanted it back.' Fingering his beard uneasily, he looked around. 'Did – was he killed here?'

'No, at King Street Public Hall just before midnight.' Thane saw him jerk with surprise and nodded. 'He was there helping build a model railway display.'

'I know.' Davidson flushed. 'I mean I – I'm in the same club.'

'And this?' Thane gestured towards the metal box.

'A radio control unit for handling models from a distance.' Davidson saw he was expected to go on, and sighed. 'With one of these you send a radio signal to your model, it picks up the signal, and obeys. This one can handle different functions on separate frequencies at up to half a mile. I was using it on a plane I built.'

'All right, but why bring it here?' queried Thane, his manner easing a little. 'Why not take it to Durman at the King Street hall?'

'Because he said something important had turned up and the best he might manage was to get there sometime.' Davidson sucked his lips and tried to explain the rest. 'I should have been at the hall myself, but I couldn't make it.'

'So when did he give you the key?'

'This afternoon. I saw him out at his car showroom – that's in a lane near King Street.'

'We know it,' said Thane dryly. 'Why couldn't you have taken the control unit to him then?'

Davidson sighed. 'Because right then I didn't have the damned thing. I'd loaned it to someone else and still had to get it back. But I didn't tell Harry that – he was in a big enough panic about needing it in a hurry.'

'Did he say why?'

'Something had gone wrong with the only other remote unit he had.' Davidson shrugged. 'He said he didn't care how late I got here, as long as I brought the thing.'

'And what were you doing tonight?' asked Thane, reaching for his cigarettes.

'I was out with a girl.' Davidson gave a wavering, self-conscious grin. 'I like model trains, Chief Inspector, but I give girls priority.'

Beech made a sudden throat-clearing noise in the background. Thane rubbed a hand across his chin, smiling a little, and tried again.

'Her name?'

'Tracy Walsh.'

Thane stifled a whistle. 'Jarrold Walsh's daughter?'

'That's right. Her old man's loaded, but she's nice with it.' Davidson seemed to feel he had reached firmer ground and relaxed a little. 'We went to a disco club in town, the Yellow Pearl. Plenty of people saw us there.'

'And afterwards?'

'I drove her home, then came straight here.' Davidson paused, stuck his hands in the pockets of his leather jacket, then added, 'Harry was the reason I got to know Tracy Walsh. I was out at his showroom one Saturday when she walked in. He introduced us – though he told me his name wouldn't be much of a recommendation to Tracy's old man.'

Thane didn't answer. But exactly why Jarrold Walsh

had chosen to become involved with a back-street trader like Durman had puzzled him at the time of the bingo hall fire – and the partnership had ended abruptly afterwards.

'Well, you'll have things to do.' Davidson interpreted Thane's silence in his own way and began to edge towards the door. 'And you won't need me, so . . .'

'Not yet.' Thane stopped him. 'Beech . . .'

'Sir?' Detective Constable Beech, waiting with a weary patience in the background, came to life.

'I'll radio for a fingerprint team and other help for you. When they come, go over the whole apartment – I don't care how long it takes.' Thane glanced at Davidson, who was frowning again. 'But while you're waiting, Beech, get our friend to run through his story again for your notebook.'

Beech nodded, remembering wryly that he'd told his wife he'd be off duty in time to help with the twins at their two a.m. feed. Well, there was always the six a.m. – if he was lucky. Two a.m. he didn't mind, but six a.m. was the one he loathed, when getting a feeding bottle into a yelling mouth was more blind, gummy-eyed luck than aimed judgement.

'Couldn't the statement thing wait till morning?' pleaded Davidson unhappily. 'I mean – well, what difference would it make?'

'You'll at least stop D.C. Beech from feeling lonely,' said Thane cheerfully. 'Good night, Mr Davidson.'

He had gone before the wisping beard had even begun twitching towards a reply.

Things had quietened when the Millside duty car returned to King Street Public Hall. The Scientific Bureau's mobile laboratory van had gone, along with most of the other cars which had been outside. A

21

solitary uniformed constable, on duty at the main door, shared his vigil with a small cluster of hopeful pressmen.

Nodding to the reporters but shaking his head to their questions, Colin Thane strode in past the constable. Inside the hall the lights still burned brightly, but again most activity seemed to have ceased. Two men he hadn't seen before, one in late middle-age and wearing a brown linen dustcoat, the other young and red-haired, were standing gloomily in the shadow of a Church Guild stall and looked up hopefully as he approached.

Then Thane winced as an all-too-familiar bark of a voice reached him from the half-opened door of the caretaker's office. He mentally braced himself for what the next few minutes were likely to bring – Chief Superintendent William 'Buddha' Ilford, head of Glasgow's C.I.D. force, was seldom affable when he had to turn out after midnight.

Pushing the door wider, Thane went in. Phil Moss was already there, draped wooden-faced against a filing cabinet. Ilford, a bulky, heavy-jowled figure with thinning grey hair, stood beside the caretaker's desk and was bellowing down the telephone gripped in his left hand.

'Yes, I agree, sir,' he grated again as Thane came in.

Glancing round, he greeted Thane with a cross between a scowl and a silent appeal, then turned his attention back to the receiver. 'Thane's here now, sir. I'll tell him.'

While Ilford listened to the reply from the other end, Phil Moss silently mouthed the words 'Chief Constable' across the room. Thane raised his eyes towards the ceiling in answer, then Ilford was barking again.

'I agree. But who'll let the police committee people . . .?' He stopped, listened again, and looked a shade happier. 'Well, I'd certainly be grateful. Right, sir. Good night.'

The receiver went down. Ilford took a chest-swelling breath, then slumped down in the nearest chair, ignoring an alarming creak.

'That, if you haven't guessed, was the Chief Constable – who isn't at his happiest,' he told Thane grimly. 'When we're landed with a headache like this I expect to be told about it direct by my divisional officers. Would you like to guess how I heard this time?'

'Sir?' Thane waited cautiously.

'From the Chief Constable, who was dragged out of bed by some reporter phoning his home. The reporter wanted to know if this damned Project Community exhibition would be scrubbed.' Ilford slammed a large, ill-tempered hand on the desk-top beside him. 'So then the Chief Constable, not knowing what the hell's going on, phones me – and I've got to fall out of bed to find out.'

'The word got around fast enough.' Thane looked as puzzled as he felt. 'Phil . . .?'

'The caretaker,' murmured Moss. 'My fault – I left him alone in here with that telephone. Daily paper rates are pretty good for murder tip-offs.'

'Well, it happened.' Ilford took out a handkerchief, blew his nose in trumpet fashion, and became slightly more amicable. 'The Chief Constable agrees the exhibition should be – well, he says postponed, I say cancelled. We'll sort that out later. He'll cope with the police committee.' He sighed and shook his head. 'Who started this damned exhibition idea anyway?'

'Divisional community relations, sir.' Thane felt a sudden pang of sympathy for Sergeant Francey Lang, already in deep enough trouble. 'It's in line with their responsibilities – "fostering police and public mutual understanding" is what the handbook calls it.'

23

'Damn the handbook and damn community relations.' Buddha Ilford pronounced the words like a
searing blasphemy, then sighed. His chin dropped on
his chest and, still slumped in the chair, he looked
down with the weary contemplative air which had
won him his nickname. 'All right, Thane – I know
the situation here. What's the score at Durman's
house?'

'A break-in, and a thorough one. Whether our
friend with the jemmy found what he wanted is any-
body's guess. But it wasn't any casual job.' Quietly,
Thane sketched the situation, paused, then added
slowly, 'I think I'll have a talk with Jarrold Walsh in
the morning.'

'Then watch your step.' Buddha Ilford looked up, a
warning in his narrowed eyes. 'I know Jarrold Walsh
from a long time back, when he skated on some
remarkably thin ice. Now – well, one wrong sugges-
tion and he'll have a lawyer at each elbow, ready to
sue on sight.'

'I'll go easy, sir.'

'Right.' Ilford slowly heaved himself to his feet.
'Thane, do I need to tell you there's a football game
coming to this city in two days' time?'

'Scotland and Holland.' Thane nodded wryly,
knowing what was coming.

The sports pages were already throbbing with forecasts for the game, a mid-week evening fixture to be
held at Hampden Stadium as a preliminary for the
next World Cup competition. Currently, the Dutch
were reluctantly quoted as favourites,

'We'll have around a hundred thousand damned
fans pouring in – maybe twenty thousand of them
mad Dutchmen,' rasped Ilford. 'That's another little
job on my plate. It could mean anything from the odd
riot to a formal declaration of war before it's over. So
get this killing cleared up fast. Understand?' He

paused, a thought striking him. 'On your own at home just now, aren't you?'

'Yes, sir. For a week or so, anyway.'

For another ten days, to be exact. The offer of a loaned holiday cottage had come from his sister-in-law and had been too much for Mary. She'd conned the local school into giving their two children time off and organized the rest. Thane had seen them off, laden with luggage, while he made noises about trying to get up for a couple of days before they returned.

There didn't seem much chance of that happening now.

'I heard somewhere.' Ilford's mouth shaped an almost sadistic satisfaction. 'Well, at least you'll have no distractions. Buy yourself a new tin-opener – that's all you'll need.'

Nodding at Moss, he stumped out of the room. A couple of moments later they heard him bellowing for his driver.

'It could have been worse,' mused Moss, scratching hard across his chest. 'When he arrived you were all set for a beat in Outer Mongolia.'

'It could still happen,' agreed Thane. 'We'd better check Durman's showroom hasn't had visitors.'

'I'll take that one.' Moss levered himself away from the filing cabinet. 'Before I go out into the night we found Durman's car parked and locked across the street from here. It's a dark red Ford – the Scientific mob have taken it over. Oh, and there's a caretaker and a club secretary outside. Want them now?'

'The caretaker first.' Thane's mouth tightened, remembering the telephone calls. 'What's his name, Phil?'

'Sam Shearer – he's been here four years.' Moss shook his head in despair. 'Now he admits there was a side door open right up until after Francey Lang

25

found the body. The club secretary is Carl Jordan – he seems decent enough.'

'Wheel in Shearer first,' said Thane grimly. 'I'll give him two minutes. But he'll remember them.'

Grinning his understanding, Moss released a low-key belch and strolled out. Another moment, and the little man in the brown dustcoat came in. He looked far from happy.

'I've heard a few things about you, Shearer,' Thane told him, an edge behind every word. 'So far, I don't like any of them.'

Visibly wilting under the first few questions, Shearer gloomily admitted that he regularly left more than one side door of the hall unlocked – often right up until the time he went home.

'But I only told a few folk,' he insisted quickly. 'It was just a wee arrangement to make life easier, mister.'

'Even after the hall was supposed to be empty?'

Shearer licked his lips and made a small attempt to justify himself.

'How was I to know a flamin' nut-case would wander in?' he protested. 'You should be out tryin' to nail him before he does for someone else!'

Thane took one long, exasperated stride across the room, grabbed the little man by the collar of the brown dustcoat, and hoisted him up till his heels were off the floor.

'Shearer, don't make it any worse!' He fought down the temptation to shake the man till he rattled. 'This whole mess happened because you were snoring in some corner.'

A sound like a squeak came from Shearer's lips and his eyes bulged with fright. Disgusted, Thane let him go.

'Out,' he ordered bleakly. 'Ask Jordan to come in.'

Still quaking, Shearer scurried out of the room.

Secretary of the Millside Tru-Scale Model Club, thirty years of age and looking slightly apprehensive, Carl Jordan was a red-haired man with a broad, freckled face. He wore a neat grey lounge suit and walked with a heavy limp.

'Sit down, Mr Jordan,' invited Thane, pushing forward a chair.

'Thanks.' Jordan settled into it, favouring his left leg, while Thane contented himself with sitting on the edge of the desk. 'I've heard what happened, Chief Inspector. If I can help, I will.'

Something in Jordan's manner didn't seem completely right. But Thane smiled and gave a small gesture with his hands.

'So far we're not so much looking for answers as trying to find questions,' he confessed. 'Apart from being club secretary, what's your regular job, Mr Jordan?'

'I'm an estate agent – well, I work for one, anyway. When I was at school I wanted to be an engineer but it never quite happened.'

'And models are the next best thing?' Thane nodded. 'How many of your club were working here tonight?'

'About a dozen.' Jordan fished a folded sheet of paper from his pocket. 'I made a list for you.'

'Good.' Thane took the sheet and glanced at it. 'Harry Durman isn't on this.'

'No.' Jordan shrugged awkwardly. 'He hadn't shown up by the time we'd finished getting things ready.'

'You didn't see him before you left?'

Jordan shook his head.

'But when we found him, it looked as if he'd been working on the track.' Thane paused and raised an eyebrow. 'How would that happen?'

'He must have come in later, I suppose.' Jordan

sucked his teeth and frowned. 'I saw where he was killed, Chief Inspector. I'd say he had just finished tidying a wiring relay – Harry Durman was the type who could always find something he reckoned wasn't right.'

'Did that make him popular?'

'No.' Jordan gave a wry grin. 'He was a fanatic on detail. But – well, he was keen, he was older than most of us, and we rubbed along with him.' He shrugged. 'There was another reason, I suppose. Harry usually had more money than most of us – more money and more equipment. He was always willing to help out.'

Thane nodded his understanding. 'What about Roy Davidson?'

'He called off for tonight.' Jordan relaxed a little and gave a soft chuckle. 'He had a date with a girl – I've seen her and I'd have done the same.'

'So you're quite sure Davidson didn't come near the hall?'

'Positive. You don't think . . .?'

'I only asked if you'd seen him.' Thane came down from the desk, took out his cigarettes and offered them. Jordan shook his head but he lit one himself and took a long draw. 'Carl, we're looking for help. Any kind of help, from gossip onward. So think a moment. Think about Durman. Has there been anything different about him lately, anything you've seen or heard?'

Suddenly, the same look of guarded apprehension was back in Jordan's eyes. He sat silent, chewing his lip a little.

'Anything,' encouraged Thane. 'Think about it. We've plenty of time.'

Jordan nodded but didn't answer.

'Carl, we're talking about a murder,' said Thane softly. He gave the red-haired man another moment,

28

then added, 'Whatever's worrying you, holding it back isn't going to help.'

'Maybe you're right.' Jordan sighed and rubbed a hand across his face. 'Durman – well, about a month ago he got me to help him with something.' Having started, the words began to almost tumble out. 'He wanted a load of electronic hardware, small stuff, transistor circuits – that sort of thing. He gave me the cash and I was to shop around for them in different places. Then – well, I was to forget about it.'

'Be glad you didn't.' Thane had the sudden feeling that at last he'd been presented with something positive. 'You got the stuff for him?'

Jordan nodded. 'The way he wanted it. In small batches, for cash.'

'So that it couldn't be traced again.' Thane nodded his understanding. 'Did you ask him why?'

'In a way.' Jordan smiled weakly. 'He told me to mind my own damned business. I – I remember some of the bits I got him. I could make a list if it helped.'

'Do that.' It still didn't make sense. 'Carl, you're a model maker. With the kind of stuff he was buying you must have had some idea what he was doing.'

Slowly, Jordan shook his head. 'Chief Inspector, I tried to find out myself. I even took one package of stuff out to his apartment, when he wasn't expecting me, more or less barged into that workroom of his.'

'And?'

'All I saw was a tangle of stuff lying on the workbench. Then he threw a dust-sheet over it. Whatever he was doing, it wasn't any kind of model-making I know about.'

'You kept on getting the stuff for him. Why?'

'There was a reason.' Grimly, Jordan pushed up from the chair and on to his feet. 'You've seen the way I walk, Chief Inspector – that was a car crash, last year. I spent six months in hospital, I came out damned nearly broke, and even though my wife took a job we were tight for cash all round. So I asked Durman if he'd help me.'

'How much?' asked Thane, in a low, weary voice.

'He gave me five hundred pounds, interest free.' Jordan limped over to the doorway and looked out towards the railway layout. 'Then – well, when he asked me to get the electronic stuff he said that if I did him a few favours I could forget about the loan.

'I couldn't afford to turn him down, Chief Inspector. In fact, I was damned glad to have the chance – till now.'

Chapter Two

It was four a.m. and raining when Colin Thane finally left the hall and had one of the divisional cars take him to Millside police station. On the way the downpour quickened till it was lashing the streets and beating a tattoo on the car roof. By the time the car reached Millside the gutters were awash and he sprinted the short distance from the car to the police station door.

Inside the brightly lit building a sergeant was yawning at the inquiry counter. Nodding to the man as he passed, brushing some of the rain from his shoulders, Thane climbed the stairway to C.I.D. territory. In the main C.I.D. room, a scatter of desks, telephones and filing cabinets, only a few of the night team were around to greet him.

They were the lucky ones and knew it, their one wish that their luck would last and they wouldn't be sent out into the downpour. For the rest of the team it was going to be a long wet night spent knocking on doors in the dull routine behind any murder investigation.

As usual, the night logbook was waiting for him. Thane checked it briefly. Millside's other problems were thankfully minor – a seaman slashed near the docks but a man in custody, a few housebreakings which could keep and a husband versus wife battle which had ended with the husband in hospital.

He told the night team's desk sergeant to hold back on anything short of an emergency, went through to his own office, and gloomily stuck a new pin on the divisional crime map where it showed King Street Public Hall.

But that was his immediate role finished. Yawning, Thane dragged out the folding camp-bed which, with a private washroom, amounted to a divisional chief inspector's status symbols. Sleep gumming his eye-lids, he slipped out of his jacket and shoes, lowered himself into the metal-and-canvas frame with its single blanket, and within moments was snoring gently. In the main office the night men heard him, grinned their relief, and began playing poker for matchsticks.

It was still raining a gentle drizzle when the day-shift orderly wakened him at seven-thirty a.m. He had shaved and dressed, and was standing by the window with a mug of tea in one hand and a half-eaten bacon sandwich in the other when Phil Moss arrived at eight. Outside, the first of the morning rush-hour traffic was splashing through the puddled streets and black, fat-bellied clouds banked the sky to the west with a promise of more weather to come.

''Morning.' Moss had shaved but had missed a patch under his mouth. He glanced at the unmade bed, twisted his thin face in a dry grimace, and tossed a batch of report sheets on the desk. 'Yours – compliments of the night shift.'

'Thanks.' Thane considered the report sheets with a jaundiced eye, bit again on the bacon sandwich, and chewed for a moment. His mouth told him he'd smoked too much the night before and his mind still felt like a flattened sponge. Another matter hadn't helped. He asked, 'Seen the morning papers?'

'Not yet.' Moss looked around.

'They're in the bucket.'

Moss retrieved two from the bundle dumped in the waste bucket, skimmed their headline page one treatments of the King Street murder, then dropped them back where they'd come from with a finger-and-thumb delicacy.

'A good start to the day,' he said sardonically.

Thane nodded a wry agreement, crossed to his desk, and sat in the big, well-worn leather armchair he'd inherited from his predecessor, who had bought it at an auction. Picking up the report sheets, he thumbed through the first few.

'Anything worth while in this lot, Phil?'

'One high note,' answered Moss stonily. 'Sergeant MacLeod stood on somebody's dog and got bitten.'

Thane grinned a little. Detective Sergeant MacLeod, bulky and middle-aged, seldom had things go right for him.

Scanned through, the report sheets came down to what he'd expected. The model engineering club members who'd been at King Street had nearly all gone straight home afterwards. The remaining few offered easily substantiated stories – and the same applied to any other helpers who'd been at the hall the previous night. Helpers they knew about, at any rate. He cursed the caretaker's unlocked doors under his breath.

'Anything through from the Scientific mob?' asked Moss, settling in a chair opposite.

'Not so far.' In itself, that was a bad sign.

'It's early enough.' Moss burped gently, reached into a pocket, and brought out a grubby, battered pill box. Opening it, he selected a large, multi-coloured pill with tender care. Swallowing the pill at a gulp, he tucked the box away again.

Thane ignored the performance. Phil Moss collected ulcer cures with a pack-rat intensity. In his room at the boarding-house he called home he had at least a drawerful of remedies tried and rejected.

The last report sheet was as dull as the rest. He shoved it aside with the others and looked up.

'Phil, what's the latest word in from Durman's car showroom?' he asked.

'All quiet, no change,' answered Moss.

The dead man's business premises had been locked and secure when the first check had been made during the night. The key-holder had been called out to make sure – and ever since two plain-clothes men had been on watch outside. But they'd had nothing to report. The last call logged from them was a plaintive query about when they'd be relieved.

'In its own way, that helps. If Durman's killer went looking for something he must have found it at the apartment.' Thane took a last gulp of tea from the mug. 'For now, I want to learn more about Durman – including this electronic caper he had under way with Carl Jordan.'

Moss nodded. 'What do we do when Jordan brings in that list of materials?'

'Shoot it straight over to Headquarters. Let the Scientific Bureau boys try and make sense of it. We've one other line which might stand checking – if Durman had worries he still didn't seem to be short of cash.'

'And that's our lot,' grunted Moss, unimpressed. 'Unless Records come up with a notion.'

'Known associates?' Thane was keeping that hope in reserve. 'We'll have to wait for that.'

Criminal Records, a department which ran itself like a private republic, seldom wasted time. But its staff couldn't be hurried, its operation depended on a thorough, almost academic, approach. Some 300,000 names were on its master files, surrounded by a maze of punch cards, cross-index systems and photo-graphic collections.

One segment was Modus Operandi, specializing in habits and methods. Another was Criminal Intelligence, weaving rumour and gossip into patterns of forecast and prediction.

They'd all be working on Harry Durman, deceased. Patiently – Thane sighed at the thought. Waiting had never been his strong point.

'So where do we start?' demanded Moss. Bringing out his cigarettes, he rolled one across the desk towards Thane, took another for himself, and accepted a light.

'Jarrold Walsh first.' The gambling club boss, Durman's one-time partner, seemed as good a beginning as any. 'Then we can have a look at that showroom . . .' Thane stopped as the telephone rang. Lifting the receiver and answering, he reached hopefully for a pencil.

''Morning, Colin.' Superintendent Dan Laurence, head of the Scientific Bureau, had a gravel-like voice which rumbled over the line from Headquarters. 'Your little friend with the sharp screwdriver – like my old mother used to say, sometimes we've good days and sometimes we've bad.'

Thane grimaced at the receiver. 'And this one, Dan?'

'Not much as far as the actual murder goes,' admitted Laurence sadly. 'A barrow-load of fingerprints all around, but I'll bet they don't get you anywhere. You know the weapon was wiped – and that's about your lot.'

Thane shook his head at Moss's silent query then asked, 'What about Durman's car?'

'We're still trying there.' Laurence's voice took on a

different edge. 'The apartment might be different, though. Like to visit Headquarters in a couple of hours?'

'Why?' asked Thane quickly.

Laurence chuckled. 'Wait and see, laddy. I might be right, I might be wrong. Either way, you'll at least see an exhibition o' brains, intelligence and enterprise. We've built ourselves a new coffee machine.'

'Dan . . .' Thane tried to keep the exasperation he felt under control.

'Patience,' soothed Laurence. 'Er . . . are you going to the Scotland–Holland game, Colin?'

'Me?' Thane laughed bitterly. 'Ask Buddha! Why?'

'Friendly conversation,' said Laurence, slightly hurt. 'That's all.'

He hung up, leaving Thane to lay down his own receiver with a curse.

'Well?'asked Moss.

'They've got hold of something. But they're being old-fashioned about it.' Thane got to his feet. 'To hell with it – we'll go and annoy Jarrold Walsh.'

'Fine.' Moss heaved himself out of his chair and reached the door first. 'Ever read the gossip columns, Colin?'

'You've got to be joking.' Thane glanced at the window, saw it was still drizzling, and collected his raincoat from its peg. 'Why?'

'Walsh had a few mentions recently,' mused Moss, opening the door. 'He's marrying again – the woman used to be a TV actress.'

'Well, we won't rate as much of a wedding present.' Thane led the way into the main C.I.D. office.

They told the duty desk sergeant their programme, then started towards the stairway which led down past Communications to street level. Halfway along,

Moss slowed and nudged Thane. Ahead, just at the top of the stairway, Francey Lang was talking earnestly to a detective constable.

The constable saw them first, muttered a warning, and Lang turned, stiffening.

'Looking for me, Sergeant?' asked Thane dryly.

Lang grinned weakly and came over. He was in his best uniform and his boots had been polished till they shone.

'Maybe it's another community relations notion,' said Moss, wooden-faced. 'We'll give you an armed guard this time, Francey.'

Lang flushed. 'No, it's not that, sir. But . . .'

'Well?' Thane treated him more kindly. 'Let's have it, Sergeant.'

'The Chief Constable wants to see me this morning.' Lang's face showed how he felt about that prospect. 'But afterwards – look, sir, I spent a long time on a beat around here. I know the people and they know me. I thought . . .'

'That you might start a one-man murder inquiry?' Thane's manner hardened and he shook his head. 'Don't be a damned fool, Francey. You've got troubles enough.'

'I could ask around.' Lang moistened his lips. 'I've still got contacts, sir. Plenty of them owe me favours.'

Thane sighed and glanced at Moss, who gave a faint shrug. Neither of them liked the idea. But Lang was right. A beat man built up his contacts on a different, often firmer relationship from that achieved by his C.I.D. counterparts.

'All right,' Thane agreed reluctantly. 'Ask around. But nothing more. Understand?'

Lang grinned his thanks.

'Say hello to the Chief Constable for us,' murmured Moss.

They didn't wait for a reply.

Somebody had robbed a jewellery shop at shotgun point over in Southern Division and Control was spluttering instructions to a whole pack of patrol cars, trying to marshal them in pursuit. But Southern Division was on the other side of the river and as long as the shotgun bandit stayed over there it was nobody else's concern. Settled in the back seat of the Millside duty car, a black Jaguar 4.2 litre, Colin Thane listened to the messages with only detached interest.

The car's screen-wipers slapping against the drizzle, its engine note a mere murmur, they weaved their way out through the traffic in unobtrusive style. Their driver, a thickset, fair-haired Viking of a man named Erickson, hummed under his breath as he steered. Watching him, Thane wondered if Erickson knew he had the beginnings of a small boil on the back of his neck, then turned his attention to Moss for a moment.

Swaying with the car's ride, looking more asleep than awake in his corner, the Millside second-in-command was utterly relaxed and looked for all the world like a thin, untidy dormouse.

Phil Moss could switch on or off practically at will – and Thane envied him that ability, one he'd spotted almost from the day that his second-in-command had arrived straight from a Headquarters desk job. It had been the same day Thane had been assigned from the regional crime squad to run Millside Division's C.I.D. – an apparently ludicrous partnership, but one which had quickly paid off.

That it worked came down to contrasts. Thane grimaced to himself, knowing his own gambling, hunch-backing nature, combined with a tendency to stretch the rules just short of breaking point, regularly had him on the verge of disaster. But that was precisely when Phil Moss came grumbling to the rescue, acting like a safety line, somehow conjuring up a second chance by slogging attention to detail.

Some men might have resented being juinor to a younger man with fewer years' service. But Phil Moss was content in his own way, the only raw spot in their relationship his complaints at the way Thane regularly neglected the divisional paperwork.

'But damn it, I'm a cop – not a filing clerk.' Thane said it aloud without meaning to, then saw Erickson glancing at him oddly through the rear-view mirror.

'Eh?' Moss stirred to life, blinking. 'Are we here?'

'Not yet.' Thane scowled back at Erickson, drew hard on his cigarette, and had one last, horrifying thought.

Suppose Phil Moss's ulcer ever caused him to fail the annual medical . . .?

Then, he decided, Millside would really be in trouble. And so would Colin Thane!

Jarrold Walsh's house was a large Victorian villa just beyond the outer fringe of Millside Division, in county territory. Tall pillars guarded its gateway, and the gravelled drive curved through neatly manicured lawns edged by immaculate floral borders. The villa, three storeys of stone elegance plus a sprawl of outhouses, had a well-painted look which came from regular and expensive maintenance.

Murmuring up to the front door, the black police Jaguar came to a halt beside its civilian counterpart – a white 4.2 with radio telephone, bright wire-spoke wheels and extra quartz-halogen spotlamps. A little way along a silver-grey Mercedes-Benz coupé looked plain by comparison.

'Wait for us,' said Thane, reaching for the door handle. 'He may throw us out – he may not. You'll soon know.'

Erickson grinned, nodded, and stretched himself into a more comfortable position behind the wheel as they left. The way he saw it, C.I.D. was a dead-end occupation. Once he got his night school law degree he'd be out of uniform and in business as a defence lawyer. That was where the money lay.

A flight of broad, stone steps took Thane and Moss to the front porch of the villa. Thane pressed the doorbell, they heard it peal somewhere deep inside, and a full minute passed before the heavy oak front door swung open. A small, plump middle-aged woman in a housekeeper's overall started to smile a greeting, then saw the police car in the background and frowned instead.

'Yes?'

'Chief Inspector Thane.' Thane showed his warrant card briefly and smiled reassuringly. 'Is Mr Walsh at home?'

'He's still having breakfast.' The housekeeper made it sound a sacred ritual. 'He doesn't see people this early.'

'There's always a first time for everything,' murmured Moss. 'Let's make his day.'

She looked at him coldly, but Moss grinned, unconcerned.

'Wait, please,' she snapped, and the door closed firmly.

'A resident dragon.' Moss looked around, reluctantly impressed by the house and garden. 'Colin, this is quite a layout. Like the old saying, the bookie never loses.'

'He's a club owner and remember it,' warned

40

Thane wryly. 'If we need, we'll lean on him later. But treat him gently this time.'

When the door opened again the housekeeper hadn't thawed. But she beckoned them in and they followed her along an oak-panelled hallway. At the far end she tapped on an inner door, opened it, and gestured them to go through.

It was a long, narrow dining-room with thick carpets underfoot. French windows ran full-length along one side and the room was furnished throughout in luxury style. Two men, one middle-aged and the other considerably younger, were seated at the breakfast table in the middle.

'Well Chief Inspector?' The older man, tall and broad-built, had iron-grey hair and heavy black-rimmed spectacles. Wearing a blue dressing gown over pale yellow pyjamas, he showed neither surprise nor curiosity at their presence. 'I'm Jarrold Walsh. I was half-expecting something like this.'

'What he means is he said he'd bet on it,' declared the younger man bluntly. He was fully dressed, wore a grey business suit, and his build and features made their relationship clear. 'I nearly took him on – I should have known better.'

'You'll learn, laddy.' Jarrold Walsh silenced him with a casual gesture. 'Chief Inspector Thane – yes, I know you.' He chuckled a little at Thane's surprise. 'We met once, briefly, years back. I think you were a sergeant then. And – ah – your friend?'

'Detective Inspector Moss – he's with me at Millside Division.' There were three settings at the breakfast table, one still to be used.

'Good. And this is my son, Frank.' Relaxed, but watchful, Jarrold Walsh waited while they exchanged nods. Then, picking up one of the newspapers beside him, he turned its headlines towards Thane. 'I'm presuming you came about Harry Durman.'

'We're asking a few people about him,' answered Thane neutrally.

'You're welcome to that.' Jarrold Walsh grimaced slightly. 'Still, sit down – both of you. Like some coffee?'

'It sounds a good idea. ' Thane pulled out one of the spare chairs and sat down. Nodding his thanks, Moss followed his example.

'Wait till you taste it,' said Frank Walsh sourly. 'You'll maybe feel differently.'

'Low caffeine and mostly milk,' sighed his father. As the younger man brought cups from a sideboard he explained wryly, 'I'm nursing a brand-new duodenal ulcer – with the questionable help of an idiot doctor who suddenly turns out to be a health-food crank.'

'And we're all suffering.' Frank Walsh brought over the cups, poured some remarkably pale coffee, and passed the result over to them. 'That'll taste as bad as it looks.'

Thane sipped and decided he was right, but Moss took a swallow and looked happy enough.

'My troubles can keep,' said Jarrold Walsh in a brisker voice. 'Now, about Harry Durman – I'll warn you now, Thane. Don't hope for much help from me.'

His son muttered agreement. 'What he means is . . .'

'What I said.' Jarrold Walsh showed a touch of impatience. 'Stay quiet, Frank, I'll handle this.'

Face reddening, Frank Walsh obeyed. Ignoring the minor brush, Thane started.

'Stage one is pure routine,' he said carefully. 'Your daughter Tracy . . .'

'Tracy?' Jarrold Walsh's eyebrows rose in surprise. 'What about her?'

'We've been talking to a student named Roy Davidson. He claims she can confirm his movements last night.'

'Davidson?' Walsh pursed his lips. 'I know him – a

42

long-haired wonder. He was here last night, late on. But what's he got to do with things?'

Thane shrugged. 'Very little. But he arrived at Durman's apartment with a package that interests us. I'd like to see your daughter.'

'Tracy's still asleep,' muttered Frank Walsh, frowning.

'Like hell she is,' snapped her father. 'I heard her padding around ten minutes ago. Go and get her down here, Frank.' He switched his attention to Thane. 'But you talk to her in front of me. Agreed?'

'If that's what you want,' Thane nodded.

Frank Walsh still hesitated. 'Let me get this straight, Chief Inspector. Is Davidson in any kind of trouble?'

'No.'

'Not unless he finds it here,' mused Moss, who'd been sitting quietly. He eyed Jarrold Walsh innocently. 'Did you know he was in the same model engineering club as Harry Durman?'

'That toy train playgroup? Yes.' Jarrold Walsh gave a grunt then glanced at his son. 'Frank, I asked you to get Tracy.'

Nodding unhappily, Frank Walsh went off. Sitting back, hands deep in the pockets of his dressing gown, the older man seemed lost in his own thoughts for a moment. Finally, he sighed.

'Thane, I don't mind helping. But there's a big difference between helping and becoming involved – and this family's not getting involved.'

'Meaning it would be bad publicity?' Thane experimented with the coffee again and decided to forget it. 'There's still the fact Harry Durman was your partner for a spell.'

'Like hell he was!' Jarrold Walsh rasped the words angrily. 'Let's get it straight, once and for keeps. All we had was an arrangement.'

Rising suddenly, he padded across to a small table

near the French windows and came back with a large framed photograph.

'There's my reason for wanting to stay out of this,' he said gruffly, handing the photograph to Thane.

A studio portrait, it showed a busty, slightly overweight but still good-looking blonde. Aged about forty, she wore a low-necked cocktail dress and her long hair was caught back by a black velvet band with diamanté trimmings. Across one corner of the photograph was written: 'Frank – with all my love, Ruth.'

The face jogged Thane's memory. Not so long ago she had appeared almost nightly on TV commercials, selling everything from detergents to credit-plan airline flights. Then, like most television faces, she had suddenly disappeared again.

'Ruth Blantyre,' said Jarrold Walsh, with a note of pride. 'We get married next month.'

'Congratulations.' Thane passed the photograph to Moss, who made a similar noise, then set it on the table beside the butter. 'What you're saying is you don't want any background mutterings at the wedding feast?'

'Right.' Walsh's lips tightened at the thought. 'Thane, my wife died ten years ago – but I never thought of marrying again till I met Ruth. And I don't want what's happened between us to be fouled up because a low-grade crook I once knew has got himself murdered.'

Moss blinked almost reproachfully. 'We weren't exactly planning to march down the aisle with you, Mr Walsh.'

'You're damned right you won't.' Jarrold Walsh slumped down in his chair again, his face bleak. 'I've two kids, both reasonably settled in their own way. Frank helps me run the clubs – he's twenty-seven, still learning, but he'll run the whole show some day. Tracy's only nineteen – what you'd call a late blessing.

She's at art school and shaping her own life. The way I see it, now's the time when I can afford to be selfish.'

'It won't work. Not on a murder case.' Thane met the gambling boss's glare squarely and impassively. It was Walsh who gave up first, glancing away with a scowl. Knowing he'd won a little, Thane kept straight on. 'We can try to go along with you. But that depends on the kind of deal we get.'

'New deck, cut, shuffle and off the top.' Jarrold Walsh gave a humourless grin. 'All right, I'll give it a try.'

'Starting with how you knew Durman,' suggested Moss.

'That goes back far enough.' The man's attitude tightened again. 'I knew him before he even started in the car trade. He grew up in the same street I did – solid, working-class tenement land. Lace curtains but a shared toilet on the landing.'

'And the bingo hall?' asked Thane.

'That was about a year ago.' Walsh's shoulders twitched in a fractional shrug. 'He came along one day and said he wanted to buy the old Sapphire Cinema and turn it over to bingo. It looked a good prospect, so I went in for a thirty per cent interest. Then later he came back and said he needed more cash.'

'So we propped him up again,' declared Frank Walsh, who'd appeared at the doorway. He came into the room quickly. 'Dad, maybe we should have our lawyer over for the rest of this.'

'And maybe I'll decide that, laddy. I happen to pay his bills,' Jarrold Walsh answered without malice. 'Where's your sister?'

'She's coming.' Frank Walsh tried again. 'Look, you're always telling me to go carefully . . .'

'And that's just what I'm doing.' Deliberately,

Jarrold Walsh glanced at his wrist-watch. 'When are you planning to leave for work?'

His son blinked. 'Work? While they're here?'

'Nobody's going to drag me off in chains,' soothed Jarrold Walsh. The notion almost amused him. 'But I want the overnight figures ready for when I get in. I can handle this end.'

'All right.' Tight-lipped, the younger man gave a curt nod then turned on his heel and went out.

A moment later the front door slammed. A few seconds more and a car engine roared to life outside and started away in a spatter of gravel.

'Temper.' Jarrold Walsh's eyes twinkled briefly. 'Now, where were we?'

'Propping up Durman,' said Moss laconically.

'Right. This time it gave me fifty-one per cent of the operation on that hall. But I left Durman running things. It was an investment, nothing more – I've bought into other places the same way.'

'Except this one burned down,' murmured Thane.

'It did.'

'And afterwards?' probed Thane.

'That's when he tried to con me over the insurance money.' Jarrold Walsh grinned coldly at the memory. 'He didn't get far – and any arrangement we had ended.'

'You'd check his accounts?' queried Moss.

'Yes. He hadn't tried anything there.' The man stopped, looked past them, and brightened. 'Hello, Tracy.'

''Morning,' came a sleepy voice from the doorway.

Half-turning, Thane started to rise. Waving him down again, a slim, pocket-sized girl with a wide, cheerful mouth, a pertly upturned nose and short, copper-bronze hair wandered sleepily towards the breakfast table. She stopped to kiss her father on the cheek, eased into her chair, then frowned at Thane and Moss with a frank curiosity.

46

'Frank said police.' Her grey eyes considered them in turn. Face bare of make-up, Tracy Walsh was in a green wool sweater and old jeans. She looked openly puzzled. 'That's you?'

'That's us,' agreed Thane, smiling a little.

She fought down a yawn and frowned again. 'Am I supposed to have done something?'

'No, but we think you can help us.'

'That's a relief. And you look human enough – though I haven't got my lenses in yet.' She yawned openly this time, found the coffee pot, poured a cup, and groaned at the result. 'Dad, this stuff is disgusting.'

'It's on my diet,' said her father mildly. 'But tell Mrs Dobbs . . .'

'Daily treasure?' Tracy Walsh shuddered. 'She's even hidden the damned frying pan.' She took a long swallow of coffee, sighed, and turned her attention to Thane. 'You said I could help. With what?'

Thane raised an eyebrow. 'Didn't your brother tell you?'

'Frank?' She shook her head and nursed the cup in both hands, looking at him over the rim. 'He just told me to get down here.'

'They're C.I.D., from Millside Division,' said Jarrold Walsh slowly. He pushed a newspaper towards her, pointing to the lead story. 'Better take a look at this first.'

'All right.' She peered at the page for a moment. They heard a startled intake of breath, then she concentrated on the print more closely. When she looked up again her face was pale.

'Harry Durman – I didn't know.' Then something close to alarm showed in her eyes. 'Dad – what's going on?'

'Routine,' said Jarrold Walsh firmly. 'Tell her, Thane.'

Thane nodded. 'Roy Davidson told us you were with him most of the evening.'

'Not most – all of it. Why?'

'He turned up later at Durman's apartment. He said he'd come to deliver a package.'

'That's right.' She nodded vigorous agreement. 'He had to do that. In fact, we nearly went there together, earlier – but we changed our minds.'

'Then maybe you were lucky,' said Moss dryly.

'Lucky?' She tried to understand.

Moss nodded. 'Somebody broke into Durman's apartment last night. Probably the same somebody who killed him at the King Street hall.'

'I see.' She took a slow, deep breath. 'But why do you want to know about Roy?'

'Just to make sure.' Thane took over again. 'He says you were at a disco in town then came out here.'

'A shade after midnight,' rumbled Jarrold Walsh. 'Ruth was here too and . . .'

Thane stopped him with a frown. 'Tracy?'

She nodded. 'That's right. Then he stayed for about an hour.'

'And you didn't see Durman at any time last night?'

'No. And Roy didn't leave me.'

'Good.' Thane smiled at her. 'Tracy, did you often see Harry Durman?'

After a fractional hesitation she shook her head. 'Not more than three or four times since . . .'

'Since my dealings with him ended,' rasped her father. 'Anything more, Chief Inspector?'

'No, that's all, Tracy.' Signalling to Moss, he rose, but glanced at her father. 'I may need to talk to you again, Mr Walsh – it could be today.'

'Try my office any time from noon on.' Jarrold Walsh pushed back his chair and rose, making no secret he was glad to see them gone. 'I'll come to the door with you.'

48

Tracy smiled a vaguely worried farewell as they left. Leading the way along the hall, her father said nothing until he reached the front door. Then, as he opened it, he scowled awkwardly.

'Thane, I've kept my part of the bargain. You'll keep yours?'

'For as long as it's a two-way trade.' Thane stepped out on to the porch. The sky was clearing and a blink of watery sunshine had won through. 'One thing I forgot to ask. How did that fire start in the bingo hall?'

'It's in the insurance report.' Jarrold Walsh's voice came bleak but rock-steady. 'There was an electrical fault.'

'Did that surprise you?'

Slowly, Walsh combed a hand over his iron-grey hair. His eyes had gone ice-hard behind the black-rimmed spectacles.

'I don't know what you mean,' he said grimly.

'It'll keep,' said Thane easily. 'Another time will do.'

Walsh nodded, stepped back, and the door slammed shut. As the sound died, Phil Moss sucked his teeth and looked unusually thoughtful.

'I'd like to know more about it,' he said pensively.

'The fire?' asked Thane.

'No.' Moss dismissed that impatiently. 'Walsh's diet. If I could get the same list . . .'

'His diet?' Thane opened and closed his mouth then launched on a brief, pungent description of Moss's more basic needs – all without straying beyond words of two syllables.

Listening, but unimpressed, Moss merely grinned, then followed him back towards their car.

Located near the centre of Millside Division, Durman Motors was down a side-street with a plumber's yard on one side and the Victoriana of a public lavatory on the other. A brightly lit stretch of plate-glass windows with a neon sign above the doorway, it advertised itself ready to meet every motoring need on easy long-term credit.

The Millside duty car reached Durman Motors at nine-thirty a.m. As it drew into the kerb, a flustered plain-clothes man made a late appearance from the lavatory entrance and hurried over. His name was Henderson, his main claim to fame the amount of time off he needed as Millside Division's only representative in the city's police pipe band.

'All quiet, sir,' he reported as Thane climbed out. 'Staff arrived as usual – they know what's happened.'

'Who's in charge?' asked Thane.

'A man Henry Benson, sir. He's the sales manager.' Henderson broke off for a moment as Moss came out of the car. But Moss ignored him, sniffed a couple of times, then went over to look at the showroom window. 'Benson isn't very happy about things but he still tried to sell me a car.'

'A real trier.' Thane grinned a little. 'Any outsiders called so far?'

'One, sir. He had a look at a car then left again.' Henderson had something else on his mind. Further down the street his own car was waiting. The driver was yawning, his arms resting on the steering wheel. 'Uh – we were off duty a few hours back, sir.'

'You can do that now,' nodded Thane.

Thanking him, Henderson headed off. Thane watched him go, wondering how many hours' overtime Durman's murder had already cost, then heard an explosive grunt from Moss.

'Look at them,' invited Moss sourly, gesturing at the cars in the showroom window. 'And they say keep death off the road! '

He was glaring at a sadly blemished coupé, the suspension visibly sagging and rust streaking its chrome. It had 'Ideal Family Buy' chalked across

50

its windscreen. Next to it, a battered little two-seater with torn upholstery was tagged 'Enthusiast's Choice'. From appearances, the last enthusiast had gone berserk with a ten-pound hammer.

'I'd feel safer on roller-skates,' said Thane, with an idea of what brakes and steering were probably like. 'Just be glad we're not buying.'

They went into the showroom. At once a thin, beaming figure with a dark suit, a gold inlay and a small moustache came bustling out from behind a glass partition. But the smile collapsed as he saw his visitors.

'More police?' It came like a groan.

'That's right.' Thane tried to look sympathetic. 'Mr Benson?'

'Yes.' The sales manager switched off charm and energy and draped himself against the nearest car. 'More questions?'

'A few.' Thane looked around. A girl was working a typewriter behind the glass partition but she was the only other person in sight. 'Things seem quiet.'

'They've been dead for weeks now.' Benson realized what he'd said and winced briefly. 'Well, hell, at least that's accurate. Not that it seemed to be worrying him . . .'

'Durman?'

Benson nodded. 'He hadn't given a damn lately.' A thought struck him. 'You know, I've got a couple of good buys in here . . .'

'No,' said Thane positively.

Shrugging, Benson glanced at Moss and saw even less future there. 'Forget it. Any idea who'll take over the business?'

'Haven't you?' asked Moss.

'I don't even know who'll pay the wages this week.' Benson rubbed a rueful finger along his moustache. 'There's nothing in his desk and his personal safe is locked – as usual.'

Silently, Moss produced Harry Durman's key-ring and dangled it suggestively. Understanding, Benson pushed himself upright.

'This way,' he invited.

Durman's office was a cubby-hole of a room located at the rear. His desk, one of the drawers lying open, had an ashtray made from an old brass shell-case and veteran car prints torn from a magazine were pinned round the walls.

'There it is.' Benson nodded hopefully towards an ancient safe sitting on a shelf. 'I suppose this is all right . . .'

'That's our worry.' Thane took the keys, found one that fitted at the second try, turned it, heard the lock give a satisfying click, and tugged the handle. The safe door swung open and exposed an interior empty apart from a small metal box, a box with wires leading to it from the door of the safe.

Suddenly the box began ticking. All three men froze – then the lid of the box flicked open and a little dummy hand shot up, two fingers raised in an unmistakable gesture.

'My God!' Benson spoke hoarsely, staring. 'I thought . . .'

'We all did.' Gingerly, Thane peered closer. 'Did he go in for practical jokes?'

'Not so you'd notice it – except for the cars we sell.' Benson swallowed hard. 'Well, that was a waste of time.'

'Wait.' For its apparent size, the safe's interior seemed oddly shallow. Reaching in, Thane tapped the back-plate. It rang hollow and he began feeling along the metal. Near the top he found a catch and when he pressed it the whole dummy back-plate fell away.

A low, appreciative whistle came from Moss. The exposed space, a few inches deep, was partially filled with neat bundles of banknotes. Beside them lay a fat leather wallet and some other items.

'Yours, Phil.' Thane passed back the wallet and explored on. Very gently, he brought out another find – half a dozen pencil-sized metal tubes strapped together by black insulating tape. 'Ever seen these before, Mr Benson?'

Puzzled, the sales manager shook his head. Carefully, Thane placed the pencil tubes on the desk. Acid detonation fuses could be temperamental. Turning back to the safe, he rippled one bundle of the banknotes between finger and thumb and estimated there must be close on three thousand pounds of a nest-egg lying in the space. A folded sheet of paper caught his eyes and he puzzled over the complex diagrams which covered most of its surface.

'Take a look, Colin,' invited Moss with a grim satisfaction. 'Things are getting better by the moment.'

He had emptied the wallet on the desk. There were three separate bank passbooks, all in the name of a John Hawkins. A British passport had Durman's photograph but was also in the name of John Hawkins and there was an international driving licence to match. The last item was a tiny chamois leather pouch.

Picking it up, Moss tipped the contents on to his palm. A dozen small, beautifully cut diamonds sparkled in the light.

'Of course, maybe he was just planning on having a holiday,' mused Moss sardonically. 'The incognito variety.'

Bewildered, Benson rubbed his moustache again, then made a sudden protesting noise as Thane started to close the safe.

'That money . . .'

'Will be collected. You'll get a receipt.' Thane relocked the safe and tucked the sheet of paper in his pocket. 'Surprised?'

'At the money?' Benson gulped. 'Hell, yes! The

whole business has been limping along. We fired two salesmen last month – I'm the only one left.'

'And the rest of the staff?'

'The girl in the other office and two mechanics in the workshop . . .'

'Right.' Thane cut him short. 'Phil, take another look around here. I'll check the workshop.'

Benson led the way again. The workshop, at the rear of the building, was grimy and low on equipment. The two mechanics were having a tea-break beside a car which was midway through a respray. They looked round as they heard footsteps and one of them, short and fair-haired, gave a sickly grin.

'Hello, Mr Thane.' He brushed a wisp of hair back from his forehead, showing tattoo marks across his knuckles. 'I'd a feelin' you'd turn up.'

'I wouldn't want to disappoint anyone,' said Thane softly. 'Even you, Bootsy.'

Bootsy Malloy was a ned – Glasgow's label for any vicious, small-time hooligan thug. His nickname came from his favourite weapons, heavy steel-toed industrial boots which could break a man's ribs with one kick provided someone else first knocked the victim down. Thane looked at him in silence, realizing the plainclothes men on watch wouldn't have recognized Malloy, whose home territory was the Northern Division. But Thane had met him one hectic night about two years back when Malloy and a squad of fellow neds had invaded Millside.

Their ambition had been to carve the ears off a Millside gang. Thane had personally come within inches of those boots until a craggy Highland beat constable had dented a baton on Malloy's skull.

'Aye, it's a pity about Durman,' said Malloy, breaking the silence with an uneasy effort. 'You'll be – well, lookin' around, eh?'

'That's how it goes.' Thane glanced at the other mechanic. He was elderly, harmless-looking, and obviously lost at their conversation. 'Been working here long, Bootsy?'

'A couple o' months.' Malloy showed a natural embarrassment at such a situation. 'It's this bird I've got now – she wants a ring on her finger an' me in a job.'

'You're not the first.' Thane still eyed him bleakly, but beckoned him a few steps from the others. 'Did Durman know about you?'

'That I'd done time?' Malloy nodded, unabashed. 'Yes, an' said he didn't give a damn. He needed a mechanic an' that was it.'

'No other reasons?'

'Meanin' what?' The man looked puzzled, then, slowly, his expression changed. 'Hey, you think he was workin' a racket, eh?'

Thane shrugged. 'Where were you last night, Bootsy?'

'With my bird an' her folks. Slept there too – on their flamin' couch.' Malloy showed his disgust at life. 'Ach. I've had the full clampers slapped on since I met her. An' as for here – if Harry Durman was on the crook he didn't cut me in.'

'You still might hear something,' said Thane quietly.

'Might.' Malloy rubbed a finger and thumb significantly and winked. 'If I do . . .'

'You'll tell me.' Thane let the words sink home. 'You'll tell me because if you don't, and I ever find out, your bird is going to be chirping alone for a long time. Understand?'

Malloy swallowed hard and nodded, knowing exactly what he meant.

Chapter Three

Glasgow Police Headquarters occupies a grim, soot-stained beehive of a building in St Andrew's Street, part of a shabby tenement area not far from the city centre and usefully close to the city mortuary and the High Court. Central Division's offices lie just across the road, and Glasgow Green, a stretch of dilapidated parkland to be avoided after dark, begins a few roof-tops away.

The Scientific Bureau's offices were located on the top floor at Headquarters, the next-best thing to an attic area. Superintendent Dan Laurence had the usual cigarette jammed between his lips and was shedding ash down his waistcoat as Thane walked in.

'Welcome to the brain bank,' greeted Laurence with his usual lop-sided grin. A big, shaggy, white-haired bear of a man, he thumbed towards his room. 'Come on through. Where's Phil Moss hiding himself?'

'Down below, trying to coax some details from Records.' Thane followed the Bureau chief through a minor maze of laboratory benches and into Laurence's room, which was in its usual state of organized chaos. 'We've got problems on the Durman murder.'

'Maybe more than you know.' Laurence didn't elaborate but waved him into a chair.

'You made hopeful noises on the phone this morning.' Thane sat down, glancing around. Something green and nasty was growing in a glass bottle beside the Bureau chief's private tin of instant coffee. A long butchering knife, labelled as a court production, had boeen propped against a rack of test-tubes which in turn was teetering on the edge of a filing cabinet. But there was nothing in sight with any apparent relation to the Millside case. 'What about it, Dan? What have you got for us?'

'Maybe the makings of a movie.' More ash tumbling from his cigarette, Laurence lowered himself into his own chair. 'Like I warned you, we've still nothing from the actual murder location. But Durman's car was – well, what I'd call interesting.' His grin altered subtly. 'Aye, and his apartment was even better.'

Thane had almost forgotten about the car. 'A red Ford, Phil said – fingerprints?'

'Only Durman's, plus some smudges. No attempt to wipe them, so it's doubtful if they'd matter anyway. But we'll take the apartment first.' Laurence frowned around, then dug out a small cardboard box from under a plastic bag containing a couple of sandwiches. When he upended the box a scatter of tiny electronic components spilled out. One hand carefully sweeping them together, he went on, 'I've a sergeant a wee bit brighter than most – though I'd hate him to know it. Anyway, he gathered these around Durman's workroom. And I got to thinking.'

Thane eyed him hopefully. 'I arranged for you to get a list of parts Durman had someone buy for him.'

'It came, about half an hour ago. And it helped clinch things.' Laurence took a moment to use the glowing millimetre stub of his cigarette as the light for a new one. 'How much do you know about electronics, Colin?'

'If the TV fails, I send for a repair man. Why?'

'There's a whole new and damned sophisticated world growing up around electronics.' Laurence shook his head for emphasis. 'Still, if you consider a man who has a fair degree of skill, then find he has been going to a lot of trouble and expense to buy a load o' bits and pieces – well, you can start making guesses. Particularly when you can check a purchase list and note the items you haven't found.'

Puzzled, Thane tried to grasp the Bureau chief's meaning. 'Durman was making a fuss about getting back a remote control unit he'd loaned out . . .'

'And that's interesting on its own. Because there wasn't a sign of another in that apartment.' Laurence tongue-rolled his cigarette to the other corner of his mouth. 'Colin, the security world is getting damned complicated. It uses electronics almost as much as locks and bolts these days. But every time someone builds an electronic gadget there's someone ready to build an answer to it.'

Thane suddenly understood and his lips shaped a silent whistle. 'Someone like Durman?'

Laurence nodded, hunching forward across the desk. 'I tried the idea on two of the best technical security brains I know. They say the same – give them half of that list of components you produced and they could build some pretty sophisticated gadgets, the kind that could go through the average electronic security system like a dose o' salts. Banks, high-class jewellery stores, safe deposits, take your pick.'

'You're sure, Dan?' asked Thane quietly, wincing at the implications.

'Sure that it's possible,' qualified Laurence wryly. 'But whether that's what Durman was doing is your department. You know that.' He rose to his feet. 'The car's easier and pretty straightforward. I'll show you.'

They left the room and again threaded their way through the main laboratory area, where a scatter of Bureau men were at work on a variety of tasks. Laurence halted at a bench where a microscope was lying idle and looked around, scowling indignantly.

'Who the hell moved those slides?' he demanded of the world in general.

'I'll get them, sir.' Grinning, a Bureau man at the next bench stopped heating a test-tube over a gas jet and came over. He pointed to a container box beside the microscope. 'In there – I thought they'd be safer.'

'How in God's name can I ever find what I want if people move things?' demanded Laurence.

The Bureau man shrugged apologetically but gave Thane a slight wink as he turned back to work. Still grumbling, Laurence took the box, fed one of the slides from it into position, and checked the microscope's eyepiece for focus. Then, standing back, he gestured an invitation.

Thane took his place and squinted through the eyepiece. The powerful magnification showed what looked like a piece of thin, irregularly marked cord. Silently, Laurence changed the slide and this time a cross-section of what appeared to be the same cord came into view.

'Well?' asked Laurence, like an examining lecturer.

'A hair of some kind.' Thane looked up. 'Human?'

'If it was, scalping would be back in fashion,' grunted Laurence derisively. 'Narrow, irregular medulla, broad well-defined cortex and irregular pigmentation – that's top-quality mink, probably from a woman's coat. There's still a trace or two of cosmetic powder clinging to the fibres.' He decided an explanation was necessary. 'We took a hand vacuum over the inside of Durman's car and collected a few of these hairs, all positively mink. Your dead man kept expensive company.'

Thane nodded. Every moment that passed Harry Durman's background was becoming more complex and puzzling. They could start trying to trace the mink's owner – but the other problem uncovered by the Bureau chief needed at least equally urgent attention.

'Dan, if you're right on the electronics side . . .'

'If?' Laurence blinked indignantly. 'I'll put good money on it.'

'And probably win,' agreed Thane ruefully. 'So we'll have to pass the word that someone may be setting up a robbery job.'

'Meaning one of us has to break the news to Buddha Ilford?' Laurence considered the prospect for a moment, grimaced, then shrugged. 'All right, I'm elected. Which takes care o' things for now. Like to try our new coffee brewer before you go? We took a couple of old specimen jars and some scrap tubing and . . .'

'I'm due to meet Phil.' Thane quickly shook his head, knowing what Bureau specimen jars could be like. 'Some other time, Dan.'

Mildly disappointed. Laurence let him go.

He'd arranged to rendezvous with Moss in the Headquarters canteen on the ground floor. As usual before noon, the canteen was busy and he found Moss sharing a table with a uniformed chief inspector from the administration staff. The chief inspector's name was Campbell, he was bald and red-faced, and his current problem was trying to organize a special recruiting campaign.

'Who wants to be a cop, anyway?' demanded Campbell, scowling as he began fastening his jacket again, prior to leaving. 'When it comes to popularity we're only one grade above tax collectors – and they get more pay and don't have to work shifts. There's even less chance they'll get their ribs kicked in. Yet I'm supposed to drum up whole squads of idiots who want into uniform. How do I do it?'

Thane made a sympathetic noise and spooned

sugar into his coffee, half-listening to Campbell's continued complaints.

They certainly needed more men. The amount of compulsory overtime having to be worked in every division was a constant headache. But there was no alternative when the force was five hundred short of its authorized strength of three thousand men.

Even rising unemployment had hardly dented that figure. Though recruits did trickle in – Thane smiled a fraction at the thought. Average age about twenty-three, average height a shade over five foot ten inches, they arrived bright-eyed and bushy-tailed, ready to put the whole city to rights. But too many bailed out again, back to civilian life and regular hours, before their probationary constable period was halfway through, while the men who did stay found themselves part of an unending battle to control a city producing a regular hundred thousand crimes and offences a year. By some miracle a one in three crime-clearance rate was achieved in the process, which was a good enough record by any city's standards. Except that the result was the prisons kept moaning they were overcrowded.

'I'll tell you my answer,' said Campbell bitterly, getting to his feet. 'Someday I'm going to find a nice, empty desert island and I'll emigrate. No more neds, no more cops, no more people – stuff them all!'

He stumped off, leaving them grinning. Thane brought out his cigarettes, lit one, saw Moss watching, and rolled another across the table at him. It went through a patch of spilled coffee in the process, which didn't help.

Grimacing, Thane handed over a replacement.

'Thanks.' Moss accepted a light and took a long draw. Then he unashamedly salvaged the first cigarette, now brown and sodden, and tucked it into his handkerchief pocket. 'It'll dry out for later. Any luck with Dan Laurence?'

'I'm not sure if luck is the word.' Thane told him what had happened and saw the thin face opposite shape a frown as he finished.

'Durman doesn't match my idea of the average mink-wearing female,' was Moss's verdict. He took a moment or two to consider the rest. 'But on this electronics thing – maybe he was building some box of tricks as a straight contract for an outside "heavy" and being killed was – well . . .' He shrugged.

'A terminal bonus?' Thane nodded at the logic. 'It's possible. Anything you can add?'

'Nothing vital or earth-shattering,' confessed Moss wearily. 'Records spent most of the time making apologetic noises. The only "known associate" detail they've got on Durman amounts to a few of the better-known bent vultures in the car trade. You'd expect that anyway – they'll be easy enough to check but it would probably be wasting time.'

He'd hoped for more and Thane's face showed it. Moss gave a mild, sympathetic belch and released his consolation prize.

'There's one item, though. Criminal Intelligence had Durman linked with Ziggy Fraser – several recent contacts reported over the past three months. In fact, they were just becoming interested in what was going on.'

'Fraser?' Thane raised a surprised eyebrow, though the information hardly matched. Ziggy Fraser he knew mainly by reputation, a violent crook with a corner in dockside theft. But Fraser's usual idea of a big job amounted to nothing more impressive than hiring some local muscle and hi-jacking a lorryload of whisky bound for export. 'All right, we'll try him.'

'And we'll be lucky if he'll admit what he had for breakfast.' Moss viewed the possibility with an inbuilt pessimism. 'But I did one other thing, on a notion. I made a main-index check on Jarrold Walsh.'

'Anything?'

Sadly, Moss shook his head. 'Except what I got from the Arson Squad boys before I came down here. The Sapphire bingo hall fire is listed as probably caused by an electrical fault, like Walsh said. But the Arson boys wish they'd known before about those acid detonators you found. They still say the fire was rigged.'

'Any insurance details?'

'All the ones that matter. The insurers were International Fidelity and the sum insured was forty thousand pounds.'

Jarrold Walsh should have collected just over half of that sum and had probably reinvested it five minutes later. But Durman's situation might have been different. Thane remembered the bank books they'd found and wondered whether they'd represented the remains of the insurance money or a first payment on the electronic deal.

He stopped himself there, frowning. Already he was accepting the Scientific Bureau's notion without reservation. And that could be dangerous.

'Let's move,' he said brusquely, rising.

'Where?' asked Moss. 'Ziggy Fraser?'

'The day shift can start looking for him. We're going to visit Carl Jordan. I want to hear what he knows about mink.'

Horizon Real Estate Ltd, where Carl Jordan was employed, couldn't be described as in mink territory. Nor could the properties it offered in its small shop window. Located in a shopping block on the western edge of Millside Division, the estate agency seemed to specialize in plain, ordinary brick-box housing and modest price tags.

It was exactly noon when Thane's car reached there and eased into a space at the kerb. He climbed out, waiting for Moss, while the car and its uniformed driver drew a few curious glances. Satisfied it wasn't a parking ticket raid, the shoppers promptly ignored them.

The estate agent's door was ajar and they went straight in. A few chairs, two desks and an office counter seemed to constitute the firm's main assets and Carl Jordan was leaning behind the counter. But the two figures facing him, listening intently while the model club secretary talked in a low voice, were a surprise.

Looking up, recognizing his visitors, Carl Jordan froze and his face paled. Puzzled, his companions turned. Copper hair brushed till it shone, Tracy Walsh wore a green wool sweater and white flared trousers. Almost guiltily removing an arm he'd had round her slim waist, Roy Davidson chewed his wisping beard. For a few seconds all three stared at Thane and Moss with expressions which seemed one stage short of panic.

The girl recovered first.

'Hello again.' Her young face managed a fairly convincing smile. 'Who are you looking for this time, Chief Inspector?'

'If he's not sure, we could draw lots,' suggested Davidson, forcing a matching grin. 'Right, Carl?'

Jordan shook his head, limped out from behind the counter, and said quietly, 'We were talking about what happened, Chief Inspector. Talking about you, in fact. You – well, you surprised us, coming in like that.'

'It looked that way. I need your help on a point, but it won't take a moment.' Pretending not to see the relief that crossed their faces, Thane glanced around. 'On your own in here?'

'My boss always takes an early lunch.'

'Then we'll be finished and gone before he gets back,' said Moss cheerfully, and drew a flicker of gratitude from the man.

64

'Want us to leave?' queried Tracy Walsh, showing no particular inclination to move.

Thane shook his head. 'I can ask all three of you at once and save time. Did Harry Durman have a girl-friend?'

'Harry with a woman?' Roy Davidson blinked then his bearded mouth quivered oddly. 'No, I wouldn't think so.'

'Then have you ever seen him with a woman, even briefly?' probed Thane. 'He lived alone, we know that. But – well, he wasn't exactly pensionable age.'

'You don't understand, Chief Inspector.' Carl Jordan showed sad amusement.

'Tell him,' sighed Tracy Walsh. 'Never mind, I will. What they mean is Harry Durman would probably have turned and started running if anything in a skirt looked twice in his direction. Even I knew that.'

Moss scratched a cautious thumbnail along the patch of stubble on his chin. 'You mean he was a queer?'

The girl laughed a little. 'Not that way. But unless there were wheels involved he wasn't interested.'

'Wheels or circuits,' suggested Thane softly.

Carl Jordan flushed, but his two companions showed no noticeable reaction. Thane tried again.

'Did Durman say anything about planning a trip abroad before long?'

They shook their heads, looking blank. Then Tracy Walsh glanced at her wrist-watch and winced.

'The time – and we haven't eaten yet,' she declared with a frown. 'I've got to get back soon. I'm working on a class project this afternoon, which means being stuck for hours in the Dutch room at Kelvingrove Art Galleries.'

'And I've a lecture I daren't miss,' said Davidson. Frowning, he combed a hand through his long, dark hair. 'Any more questions, Chief Inspector?'

'I'm finished,' Thane told them.

'Good.' Davidson looked relieved. 'I've exams coming up soon. I can't afford to skip too many lectures.' He glanced at Jordan. 'Want to come for a sandwich, Carl?'

Jordan shook his head. 'I'm here till the boss gets back. Then I'll go home for lunch – my wife leaves something ready.'

'All right if we go?' asked Tracy Walsh.

Thane smiled and nodded. 'I'll even offer you both a lift part of the way.'

'No need. I've got my car – but thanks anyway.'

Taking the girl's hand, Davidson headed towards the door. 'See you later, Carl. Maybe you too, Chief Inspector.'

They went out. As the door sighed shut, Carl Jordan made a half-hearted show of tidying some mortgage leaflets on the counter.

'Nice kids, both of them,' he said suddenly. 'Under that long hair, Roy is damned clever. And Tracy paints like she was born with a brush in one hand.'

'They've got a few things going for them,' agreed Thane quietly. He took a casually interested glance at a display board, noting that most of the houses it offered were already marked as sold. One small bungalow was almost identical to his own in size and appearance but the price tag below made him wince. 'How's business here?'

'Pretty good – I wouldn't mind being on commission.' Jordan grimaced wryly. 'Still, I get a regular pay-cheque.'

Thane nodded. 'One thing I forgot, Carl. When you were buying that electronic stuff, did Durman ever mention a man named Fraser?'

'Fraser?' Jordan frowned a moment, then shook his head.

They said goodbye and left him. Outside, as they headed back towards the duty car, a horn blared and a small open two-seat MG of uncertain vintage pulled away from the opposite kerb. Davidson was at the wheel and Tracy Walsh waved from the passenger seat as they slotted into the traffic.

'Stayed to make sure we left too,' grunted Moss cynically. He fished a stomach pill from his pocket, flicked it from his thumb into his mouth and grinned without humour. 'They didn't like it when we walked in.'

On an impulse, Thane glanced back. Carl Jordan was at the window of the estate agency. The man gave a weak smile and retreated quickly.

Moss chuckled thinly. 'He's worried all right.'

'But not about what we asked.'

Reaching their car, Thane opened the door, gestured Moss aboard, then followed him in. Behind the wheel, Erickson shoved a football magazine out of sight and thumbed towards the radio.

'Control called us, sir,' he reported laconically. 'Headquarters wanted to know where you were. No message.'

Thane nodded resignedly. By now Dan Laurence would have told Buddha Ilford his theory about the electronic gear bought by Harry Durman. It must have made a fascinating few minutes – and Chief Superintendent William Ilford's reaction to the news wouldn't have been happy.

'Do we call them back?' queried Moss.

Thane shook his head. 'Millside,' he said bleakly.

He had enough trouble on his plate without looking for more.

There was something different from the usual in the atmosphere at Millside Division's C.I.D. office. Colin Thane sensed it the moment he entered, puzzled at the sly grins he saw slide across the faces of several of the day-shift men, and wondered exactly what was going on.

He was on his own. Phil Moss had taken the duty

car and was on his way to tap the dockside grapevine for news of Ziggy Fraser. That might not be easy. When a murder hunt was on most neds with sense vanished into the woodwork on general principle and stayed there till things cooled down again.

The grins around seemed to grow as he walked straight through towards his room. Even the normally solemn Detective Sergeant MacLeod, taking his turn as desk sergeant, looked almost sheepish.

'Well?' asked Thane. 'What's going on?'

'Ah . . . nothing, sir,' said MacLeod uneasily. 'Except . . . well, you've a visitor waiting.'

'Who?' asked Thane suspiciously. 'If it's Buddha Ilford . . .'

'No, sir.'

'Well?' Glancing over MacLeod's shoulder, he checked the occurrence book. Things seemed quiet enough in the division. 'What's the mystery?'

'It's that television woman, Ruth Blantyre. You know, sir. The – ah . . .' MacLeod frowned, searching for the word.

'Pin-up?' suggested Thane dryly.

MacLeod flushed. 'Ach, she's maybe a shade past that, sir. But she's still a damned good-looking hunk o' a woman. Her brother's with her – I put them in your office.' He saw Thane's eyebrows rise and gestured at the other men around. 'It was that or having this lecherous shower crawling over her.'

'Gallantry lurks in the strangest places.' Thane understood the grins at last but kept a straight face. 'All right, Mac, what else has disturbed your rest?'

'Chief Superintendent Ilford called. So did Francey Lang – twice, then he said he'd come in and see you. And Doc Williams delivered the post-mortem report on Durman. It's on your desk, sir.'

'Right.' Thane thumbed at the day-shift men. 'Tell them the show's over and get them out of here. We're still trying to find Ziggy Fraser.'

He left MacLeod trying to make appropriate noises and went into his room. The moment he opened the door a waft of expensive perfume met his nostrils and the source, a shade plumper than in the portrait Jarrold Walsh had showed him, smiled up from a chair beside his desk.

'Your sergeant said it would be all right if we waited in here, Chief Inspector,' said Ruth Blantyre in a huskily apologetic voice. 'You don't mind?'

'No – I'm glad.' Thane found himself grinning idiotically at her and realized the blockbuster effect she'd created outside.

Maybe Ruth Blantyre looked a few years older without benefit of studio lights. But MacLeod was right – she was a particularly good-looking and amply built woman. A pastel blue linen dress hugged her figure to everyone's advantage, a lightweight white coat was draped casually over her shoulders. She sat demurely, blonde hair styled in an immaculate coiffe, her only jewellery a plain gold necklet and an engagement ring with a solitaire diamond.

'I nearly changed my mind twice on the way here and turned back.' She smiled in a way which could have convinced most men that would have been a disaster. 'But – well, it's important to talk to you. If you'll let me?'

'That's why I'm here. I get paid to listen.' Thane knew he was grinning stupidly again. But under such close-quarters attack he was unable to do anything about it – except wonder how MacLeod had stopped the day-shift from storming their way past him.

'Good.' Ruth Blantyre took a deep, hypnotizing breath of relief then switched to a friendly, white-toothed smile. 'Chief Inspector, this is my brother, Don . . .'

Until then, Thane had hardly noticed the other figure in the room. Slim built, sallow and dark-haired,

Don Blantyre looked as though that might often happen to him. A few years younger than his sister, he had large ears and a receding chin. He came over smiling. His suit was hand-tailored and he had suede shoes and a red silk bow tie.

'You're busy, Chief Inspector – we know that,' he said in a soft voice which had a hard-to-place accent. 'And believe me this was totally Ruth's idea. I don't even know if it's a good one.'

'But I won't need more than a couple of minutes, Chief Inspector. I promise that.' She looked anxious for a moment.

'I've got time.' Thane peeled off his raincoat, tossed it on the peg behind the door, and went over to his desk.

Settling into the leather armchair, the scent of her perfume tantalizing his nostrils, he dragged out his cigarettes in self-defence and offered them.

Don Blantyre shook his head. But Ruth took one, leaning far forward towards the flame of Thane's lighter and cupping her hand round it without quite touching his own. The diamond ring winked wickedly in the sunlight streaming through the window behind her brother.

'So how can I help?' Thane tried to sound businesslike.

'You know I'm engaged to Jarrold Walsh.' She made it a statement, drew on the cigarette quickly and almost nervously went on, 'Jarrold called me and told me about this morning – and what happened last night.'

'Does he know you're here?' asked Thane mildly.

'Hell, no!' Her eyes widened at the idea, then, seeing Thane's surprise, she gave a throaty, apologetic chuckle. 'And, come to that, I don't want him to find out later.'

'Then he needn't.'

'Thanks.' She drew on the cigarette again, a faint

frown creasing her forehead. 'I was at Jarrold's place last night when Tracy came back with that Davidson boy. So if you need any confirming evidence . . .'

'We've got enough. But I think he'd appreciate knowing.' Thane waited, sensing the actress was only easing towards her real reason for coming.

'Well, that's fine then.' She pouted her lips slightly, then glanced at her brother for support. 'The other thing is that – well, you already know Jarrold and I will be married in a few weeks' time. And now Jarrold's worried sick about this happening.'

'He didn't seem that way to me,' countered Thane mildly.

'Then he put on a better act than he thought.' The blonde actress tidied the edge of her skirt a fraction, choosing her words with care. 'It will be a second marriage for both of us. He – well, Jarrold matters a lot to me.'

Her brother groaned. 'Ruthy, for God's sake get round to it before we get thrown out of here.' He gave her a moment, then shrugged. 'All right, I'll start it off. Chief Inspector, I'm Ruth's business manager. Right now I've a deal lined up for a whole twenty-six-week series of commercials with a food firm – we'll play the mature bride angle for all it's worth.'

'Depending on what's meant by mature.' Ruth Blantyre's eyes flashed dangerously in his direction, then she swung back to Thane. 'Don's right – but you've got to believe me, I don't give a damn about the deal. Not the way he does. I've a brother with a mind that calculates percentages.'

Don Blantyre shrugged, unperturbed. 'Family stuff – that's for later. Ruthy, tell the man.'

'All right.' She clenched her hands, the engagement ring sparkling anew in a lancing beam of sunlight from the window. 'There's something I want you to know, something Jarrold won't tell you. About a week ago Jarrold arrived at the Silk Slipper one evening to find Harry Durman waiting for him in his office. He tried to put the bite on Jarrold for money – and Jarrold knocked him down, then threw him out.'

'Telling the world around, "I'll murder that bastard if he shows his face here again,"' murmured Don Blantyre with a wry smile. 'Right, Ruthy?'

She nodded silently.

'You think he meant it?' asked Thane quietly.

'No.' Her head came up angrily. 'But I'm telling you now before you find out some other way. And I was with Jarrold every moment of last night – so he couldn't have been involved.'

'You were right to come,' said Thane, with a growing liking for the jungle-like loyalty he sensed beneath Ruth Blantyre's exotic exterior. 'You say Durman tried to squeeze money out of Jarrold Walsh. How? I got the impression that wouldn't be easy.'

'I don't know.' She shook her head. 'Jarrold wouldn't say – but I know what Durman tried to do before.'

'When he tried to grab most of the insurance money after the bingo hall fire?'

She nodded. 'A fire that Jarrold swears he must have started – because Harry Durman had been pressuring Jarrold to either buy him out or agree to sell the hall and take a loss. The place wasn't making money, but Jarrold wanted to hang on. Durman didn't.'

'Who told you that?'

'Jarrold.'

Thane glanced at Don Blantyre, who nodded agreement.

'Well, now we know it helps,' said Thane. He sat back and deliberately switched to an easier aspect. 'How long have you known Jarrold Walsh?'

Ruth Blantyre relaxed a little and smiled wryly. 'Since just before last Christmas. Don and I went to the Silk Slipper for a night's celebration and – well, we met.'

'Celebration?'

'She'd just been paid for a job,' explained her brother dryly. 'We'd been waiting on the money – so had a lot of other people, like bill-collectors.'

'Anyway, that's when I met Jarrold.' Ruth Blantyre fingered the engagement ring, her voice softening. 'Like Topsy, things just grew – we both liked what we saw.'

'And with the dress she was wearing that night he saw plenty,' added Don Blantyre with a caustic edge.

The telephone rang. Making a murmur of apology, Thane lifted the receiver and answered. A hoarse, aggressively determined voice sounded in his ear. Either Bootsy Malloy didn't like telephones or the fair-haired ned was far from happy about making the call.

'Thane, maybe I've remembered a couple o' things you'd find useful. But if they matter, what's in it for me?'

'No promises, Bootsy.' Thane's free hand scooped up a pencil and collected an envelope which had been lying on the desk. 'But you wouldn't lose on it.'

'Mister, I need more than that.' Malloy's heavy sniff of distrust came rumbling over the wire. 'I'm not goin' to talk myself into a cell for you or anyone. But I was thinkin', like – with that bird of mine I'm not lookin' for trouble. Anything I did was straight, ordinary work. Right?'

'If you say so,' murmured Thane. 'Nice to hear you're an honest citizen.' He grinned at Malloy's terse, one-word reply. 'Let's have it.'

'Not like this, mister. An' I'm not walkin' into any police station.'

'Then where?' Out of the corner of his eye Thane

saw Ruth Blantyre stub her cigarette and nod as her brother whispered in her ear. 'You name it.'

'I'm on my lunch-hour an' phonin' from outside. Didn't want any of that shower at Durman's place to know . . .' Malloy paused, then gave a grunt of odd amusement. 'Right, I'll tell you. Drive along past the Kelvingrove Art Galleries, but slow. I'll be near the bus stop.'

'Why there?' Thane had a sudden memory of Tracy Walsh and her art school project. 'That's out of the division and . . .'

'I've a damn good reason,' said Malloy shortly. 'Fifteen minutes, mister – if I don't change my mind before then.'

His receiver went down hard. Slowly, frowning, Thane replaced his own, then realized Ruth Blantyre had risen from her chair.

'We'll go now, Chief Inspector.' She pulled the white coat more firmly round her shoulders. 'But – well, I've changed my mind about one thing. I'm going to let Jarrold know I came here.'

'And tell him from me he should be grateful.' Thane came over and opened the door to the main office. 'He's a lucky man – luckier than he knows.'

'Thanks.' Suddenly she stepped closer, kissed him warmly on the cheek, smiled, and went out.

'Big sister's the emotional type,' said Don Blantyre dryly.

He shook hands with Thane, his grip light and casual, then headed after her. They passed an appreciative audience in the outer office, then disappeared down the stairway.

'Mac . . .' Thane's voice brought things back to normal.

'Sir?' Detective Sergeant MacLeod came over at a trot.

'I want a car out front straight away, with a plain-clothes driver. You'd better come too.'

MacLeod nodded and, as usual, didn't ask questions.

Going back into his room, Thane frowned at the notes he'd scribbled, then realized the envelope he'd used was still sealed. His name was on the front – it was Doc Williams' post-mortem report on Durman.

Ripping the envelope open, he read the single sheet inside, skimming over the usual formal phrasing of the introduction. The kernel was in the police surgeon's last paragraph.

'Subject was killed by a single stab wound which, as described above, penetrated the heart. On the basis of penetration achieved by the peccant weapon a considerable degree of force was used. But in itself this would not appear to be beyond the capability of any individual, man or woman, of normal physique.'

Doc Williams was leaving it wide open, spelling out that he'd absolutely nothing to contribute.

Yet maybe, without knowing it, he had.

Grim-faced, Colin Thane tucked the report sheet under his ashtray, lit a cigarette he knew he really didn't want and left. As he started across the main office, someone he could have done without moved eagerly into his path.

'Sir.' Francey Lang's thin face gleamed hopefully.

'Not now, Francey,' Thane told him curtly. 'Another time.'

'But, sir!' The community relations sergeant made a determined protest. 'I've heard something . . .'

'Later.' Thane made it almost a snarl and brushed past him.

Francey Lang sighed, watched him stride away and decided anyone with sense would steer clear of that tall figure until his present mood had changed.

Owned by the city and located on the edge of Kelvingrove Park, Glasgow's principal Art Gallery and Museum is a great red sandstone sprawl of a building which was built at the turn of the century. It rates as an extravagant architectural stepping stone between the classical lines of Glasgow University on the hill above and the frankly wedding-cake style of the nearby Kelvin Hall with its circus arena.

Cynics describe the Art Gallery as midway between two collections of animals and prefer the ones in cages. But the city stays proud of its Art Gallery, even if only a minority of the population venture inside. The main showpiece is Salvador Dali's vast master-piece of Christ on the Cross. But being Glasgow, the rest cheerfully extends from a nationally famed collec-tion of European paintings to medieval armour, a stuffed tiger and a display of model steamships.

Traffic was light when the Millside car turned into Dumbarton Road and the Art Galleries appeared in silhouette ahead. Thane was in the front passenger seat beside the plain-clothes driver, MacLeod was behind him, and all three men scrutinized the pave-ments on either side as the car cruised along.

'There he is!' Thane spotted Malloy first, standing near a bus stop on the opposite side of the street and wearing a green and white zip jacket over his work-ing overalls. 'Pull in.'

As they stopped at the kerb, the width of the road separating them from Malloy, the man gave a brief gesture of recognition, waited till a bus and a truck went past, then began strolling over.

He was not quite halfway when a grey Volkswagen delivery van parked ahead suddenly began moving. Accelerating savagely, engine howling, it rocketed forward. Malloy heard the engine-note, glanced round quickly – then made a frantic, horrified effort to get clear.

Deliberately, the Volkswagen altered course. The fair-haired ned, still trying to run clear, stared towards Thane with his mouth shaping a scream of terror. A second later the vehicle hit him and he became a cartwheeling rag bundle of arms and legs, catapulting through the air, then hitting the road again and rolling over and over towards the gutter.

Before he had stopped, the Volkswagen had swerved back on its course. As it passed, still gathering speed, Thane glimpsed two men in the driving cab. Their faces were a blur beneath stocking masks and they wore grey dustcoats.

Two hundred yards down the road, while the Millside car began a vicious, tyre-screaming U-turn in pursuit, the van skidded, swayed into a side-street and vanished. Wrestling with the steering-wheel, Thane's driver missed another car by a hairsbreadth, jammed his foot down to the floor on the accelerator, and held each gear to its limit.

They reached the side-street in time to see the grey van vanish down another at the far end. When they got there the driver had to brake hard, spinning the wheel and taking to the kerb to avoid a group of children standing open-mouthed in the middle of the road. A headlamp glass shattered and metal crumpled as they brushed a lamp-post, stalled, and lost vital seconds.

As they got going again, Thane had the radio microphone out and began calling Control on a red priority. But, as Control answered, the driver swore bitterly and dropped a gear.

The grey van lay abandoned ahead, doors lying open, and the tenement street was empty.

Thane and MacLeod scrambled out as the Millside car stopped beside the van. A dozen open entries offered a mocking choice through the blocks of houses around, entries they knew led to inevitable, inter-locked backyards and alleys where a hundred men could vanish.

There wasn't much hope, but they had to try. Splitting up, Thane taking one side of the street and

MacLeod the other, they spent several minutes attempting to at least find someone who had seen the men run off. It was useless and, as two traffic patrol cars arrived, Thane gave up. He left the traffic crews the equally hopeless task of cruising the neighbourhood while the Millside car took him back to Dumbarton Road.

A small crowd had gathered in their absence. Pushing his way through, Thane found a Marine Division constable busy passing a message on his personal radio. The man finished, tucked the radio back in his pocket, then stiffened as he recognized Thane.

'Called an ambulance?' asked Thane.

Silently, the Marine constable shook his head and stepped back while Thane knelt beside the broken huddle in the gutter.

Blood streaking from nose and mouth, jaw hanging slack, Bootsy Malloy lay with blank, dead eyes staring up at the cloudless sky. Whatever he'd known, the fair-haired ned had represented a risk in someone's book – a risk now totally eliminated.

A new, ice-cold anger filled Thane as he got up, brushed the dirt from his trousers-knees, and faced the silent, staring crowd.

'Did he manage to say anything?' he asked the Marine Division man, who hadn't moved.

'He was dead when I got here, sir.' The constable hesitated. 'I've advised our own C.I.D. – they're on their way.'

Thane nodded his understanding. Officially, Bootsy Malloy's murder was Marine Division property. One they'd probably have been glad to do without.

'Can anyone tell me who reached him first?' he appealed to the crowd.

They looked at each other then a stout, elderly woman carrying a shopping bag pushed her way forward. Her grey hair was in a wisping, old-fashioned bun and a button missing from the front of her shabby black coat had been replaced by a safety pin. But her lined face showed a mixture of compassion and anger.

'I did, son.'

Thane had the feeling she'd greet anyone under pensionable age that way.

'Did he say anything?' he asked.

'Aye.' She nodded, frowning. 'Just before he died.'

'Try to remember, ma,' he told her soberly. 'It could be important.'

'I doubt it.' She shook her head. 'He just muttered away about a bird – a "wee bird". That's all. The soul wouldn't know what he was saying, son. There wasn't as much as a pigeon around.'

Thane sucked his lips and nodded. 'He meant another kind of bird, ma. His girl.'

The woman sighed her understanding and slowly fumbled under her shabby coat. Stooping, she gently placed a cheap metal crucifix on Malloy's chest. Then, without another word, she turned away.

As if it was a signal, the crowd began to disperse. Out on the fringe, Thane recognized a face. For a brief instant Tracy Walsh's frightened eyes met his own. Then, just as quickly, she had gone.

Chapter Four

Detective Chief Superintendent William 'Buddha' Ilford ruled Glasgow's detective force from an unpretentious room on the ground floor of the Central Division buildings. The minute's walk which separated the Central building from Headquarters, where he would have been more logically located, was a deliberate protective moat against the administration branch and he had one other line of defence. His secretary was young, red-haired, and known to attend karate classes on her day off.

A radio summons through Control brought Colin Thane to Ilford's office at four p.m. He'd been expecting it and the kind of reception he'd receive. When he entered the room Buddha Ilford was hunched scowling behind his desk with Dan Laurence sitting to his left. The Scientific Bureau chief, the usual cigarette between his lips, managed a quick sympathetic grimace but Ilford's greeting came down to a grunt and a nod towards a vacant chair on the other side.

Thane took the chair and waited. For almost a minute Ilford said nothing, his large face stony while he fingered a flick-knife souvenir he used as a letter-opener. Then, at last, he tossed the knife aside, sat back, and spoke in a blistering rumble.

'Do you know what I'm wishing right now, Thane? I'm wishing I'd never heard of Millside Division –

that I could chop it clean off the map and lose it once and for all.'

Ilford stopped to draw breath, still scowling. 'Next time you arrange to meet an informer let me know. We'll send out tickets for the performance.'

Thane said nothing. He'd heard pretty much the same, but in more despairing tones, from his Marine Division opposite number. Marine Division C.I.D. would have to carry the statistical can for Bootsy Malloy's murder – and were far from pleased about it.

'What's the score with it now, Colin?' asked Dan Laurence mildly, breaking the threat of another silence. 'Any progress?'

'Not much. The van was stolen two hours before, the men who were in it didn't leave fingerprints and all we've got is a stocking mask dropped about two streets away from where they abandoned the thing.'

'Witnesses?' asked Ilford.

'Only one worth while, sir. He says the van appeared about five minutes before Malloy was run down.'

'So they were following him.' Ilford pursed his lips. 'Probably just waiting their chance, which he gave them when he started across that road. All right, what are you doing about it?'

'Trying to backtrack on Malloy's movements, sir. I've switched Phil Moss on to finding Malloy's girl and I've every spare man I've got working on locating this ned Ziggy Fraser.'

Apparently, Ilford couldn't think of anything to add to that. Nodding curtly, he made an abrupt switch.

'You've seen Jarrold Walsh?'

'Yes, sir.' Briefly, Thane described what had happened and saw from Ilford's face that the C.I.D. chief wasn't particularly impressed.

'In case you don't know it, anyone trying to get a

casino licence in this country has to be as pure as a blasted archbishop,' snarled Ilford as he finished. 'I helped check out Walsh myself when he was starting.'

'Which was a few years ago,' mused Dan Laurence. 'And even the occasional archbishop goes bent.'

Ilford wasn't amused. 'If he's bent, we take him. But we'll be damned sure of our facts first, and for the moment I'm more interested in Durman himself – for obvious reasons. Thane, that passport you found hasn't been used so far, the bank accounts are genuine and' – he sighed and glanced at Laurence – 'all right, you tell him your part.'

'What Durman was workin' on?' Laurence nodded and sat back, stuffing his hands in his trousers pockets. 'Colin, ever heard of a ghost pulser or a loop kill?' He grinned at Thane's blank reaction. 'Then how about a vibration desensor?'

'I said tell him,' snarled Ilford. 'Never mind the fancy trimmings.' He glanced at Thane, thawing in irritated sympathy. 'If there's one thing I can't stand it's a damned jumped-up plumber who tries to pretend he's a scientific genius.'

'The average schoolboy would understand,' said Laurence indignantly. 'But if that's how you want it, I'll try.' He drew a deep breath. 'Right now the two basic versions of electronic security hardware work on either a sensitivity to outside vibration or by objecting when anything interferes with a sort of pulse-beat the unit creates for itself. Follow me?'

Slowly, Thane nodded.

'Good.' Laurence nodded sardonic approval. 'What it amounts to is you can have a thing the size of a small can of beans lying in the middle of a room. A thing so sensitive it will react to the way the air currents in a room are disturbed if someone as much as raises an arm. No photo-cell beams, no wires – it's like my wife, damned sensitive to draughts. The second type are the vibrators. They're wired on a circuit to a door or maybe the windows. They send out their own pulse beat on an exact frequency – and if anything upsets that beat, alarms start ringing. You'll get plenty of sophisticated variations from electronic locks onward, but the principle's the same.'

'And in Durman's case?' Thane glanced at Ilford, frowning. 'He was anxious to get hold of that remote control unit . . .'

'And it looks like whoever killed him needed it just as badly,' said Ilford, cutting him short. 'We've reports of two separate break-ins at shops closed over the lunch-hour today. Both stock electronic gear. Both have lost remote control units.'

'They're being pushed for time,' mused Laurence. 'Colin, I won't pretend I understand the remote control side of this. But I'm damned certain Durman was building a ghost pulse unit – a gadget to superimpose a matched pulse on an electronic guard unit. With one of them, it is easy enough to snuff out an alarm system without giving it a chance to even sneeze.'

Thane sucked his lips hopefully. 'That should narrow things down.'

'That's what I'm hoping,' muttered Buddha Ilford. 'There's a general alert out to all forces. The Regional Crime Squad are warning every firm listed as having electronic protection, with the insurance companies helping. But – well, here's what we're up against.' He lifted several stapled, typewritten sheets of paper and tossed them towards Thane's side of the desk. 'That's the list for this city alone.'

Ilford and Laurence sat silently while Thane flicked over the pages. From diamond merchants through banks to high-security defence plants, over three hundred locations were tabulated. Finishing, Thane laid down the list and looked at Ilford knowing it would be impossible to maintain a watch on even half that number.

'It's not as bad as it looks.' Ilford allowed himself a fractional twist of a smile. 'We've got it down to about sixty locations where vibrator units are the main protection and what's being guarded really matters. One or two are in your division – you'll be getting details.'

'But there's someone a damned sight more clever than the average ned behind this,' mused Dan Laurence. 'Clever – and ruthless.' He glanced at Ilford. 'And with money to set it up. I'd go along with the idea that we shouldn't forget Walsh.'

Ilford scowled but before he could answer the telephone rang. He scooped it up, answered, then grunted and held the receiver towards Thane.

'For you – it's Moss.'

Taking the receiver, his audience waiting impatiently, Thane hoped that Phil Moss had managed to come up with something that mattered.

'Think you could escape from Buddha's clutches for a spell?' asked Moss's metallic voice over the wire. 'I'm in Columba Street – know it?'

'Yes.' Columba Street was near dockland, old property scheduled for early demolition. But it wasn't one of Millside Division's particular problem areas – trouble there usually meant the odd Saturday night brawl after the pubs had emptied. 'What have you got, Phil?'

'That "bird" Bootsy Malloy told you about.' Moss's voice took on a grimmer note. 'I had to tell her what happened and she took it pretty badly. But – well, she might talk to someone else now. Like to have a try?'

'I'll come over.' Thane hesitated. 'Phil, how about Ziggy Fraser?'

'No luck yet,' admitted Moss ruefully. 'But Francey Lang reckons maybe he can help find him.'

'He would,' sighed Thane. The community relations sergeant was beginning to constitute a problem of his own. 'Where's Lang now?'

'Prowling,' answered Moss succinctly. 'If we're lucky he'll maybe vanish down a drain.'

'He'd only bob up somewhere else. All right, give me ten minutes.' Thane put down the receiver and turned to Ilford. 'It's Malloy's girl, sir – we've located her.'

'Then maybe he told her more than you managed to get out of him,' said Ilford icily. 'Let me know – I'll be with the Chief Constable sorting out arrangements for tomorrow's damned football game. Why couldn't the Dutch have stuck to building dykes?'

It was five p.m. and dulling a little when Thane's car reached Columba Street. His driver had to slow to crawl past the noisy groups of children playing in the roadway and it was a long time since he'd seen so many dogs sniffing their way around one short street. The buildings were drab and grey, except where they'd been chalk-marked. Most of the windows were open, women leaning out of them in the tenement tradition of having a gossip with their neighbours before it was time to make the evening meal.

Thane grinned tolerantly as one small, grubby-faced boy yelled a startling obscenity directed at the police car and its occupants. Soon Columba Street would vanish, its families would be re-housed – and even if the kids stayed grubby they'd then have a bath to be dumped in at night.

It was taking time and money, but very slowly the city was beginning to win on social terms, wiping out the conditions that bred neds. It might take a couple of generations to see the final result but at least it was happening.

Every window had its spectator about halfway down the street, where the other Millside car was parked. Phil Moss stood beside it and came over as Thane's car pulled in and he climbed out.

'In there, top floor.' Moss thumbed towards the nearest entry. 'Her name is Rose Hodge, aged about twenty – works in a grocery store. She arrived home just before I got here.'

'Who's with her, Phil?' asked Thane.

'Her mother.' Moss grimaced at the memory. 'An old battleaxe, but decent enough. Her father's at work and won't be back for a spell.' He rubbed a speculative hand across his chin. 'The girl took it badly, like I said. But maybe we could try now.'

They went into the building, the entry close dark and smelling of damp and the stairway from there badly worn. An empty beer can lay on the first landing and some ritual obscenities on religion had been chalked on the second. By the time they reached the top floor Moss was panting for breath and cursing, but he recovered enough to indicate a door on the right.

It opened before Thane could reach for the bell-push. The woman who looked out was fat, grey-haired and about fifty and her face was far from friendly.

'Again?' she asked balefully, giving a brief glare of recognition towards Moss, then switching her attention to Thane. 'Mister, I don't give a damn who you are – my lass has had enough without more big-booted polis tramping in on her.'

'Either we talk to her here or at a police station,' said Thane grimly, sensing only the direct approach was going to work. 'Your choice, Mrs Hodge.'

For a moment the woman stayed where she was,

barring the door, apparently still determined. Then, suddenly, she sighed, shook her head, and stood back.

'All right,' she surrendered. 'But he wasn't worth this – damn him.'

They found Rose Hodge in the kitchen, sitting huddled in a chair beside a big, old-fashioned metal cooking range. There were cracks in the walls and a damp patch halfway across the ceiling, but the kitchen itself looked and smelled clean. Going in ahead of them, her mother took up a sentinel position beside the girl, who was dark-haired and wore a short-sleeved blue cotton dress.

'More polis,' said Mrs Hodge wearily. 'Do you want to talk to them, lass?'

Rose Hodge nodded and turned to face them. She was thin-faced, attractive rather than pretty, and her eyes showed she'd been crying.

'This won't take long, Rose,' Thane told her quietly. 'Just a few questions, then we'll go. All right?'

'If it helps.' Her voice was little more than a whisper.

'Good.' Thane nodded encouragingly. 'Bootsy told me about you, Rose.'

'Bootsy? His name was Peter,' commented her mother with a sniff. 'Or so he told us. Along with a great line o' patter about goin' straight.'

'Maybe he was trying.' Thane kept his attention on the girl. 'The way he talked, it mattered.'

'He promised he would.' Rose Hodge's small hands tightened knuckle-white, a low, bitter edge in her voice. 'Not everybody believed him – not here, anyway.'

'If he was going straight how did he get himsel' murdered?' demanded her mother defensively. She pointed an irate finger at Thane. 'An' understand this, mister. You're not involvin' our Rose in it – not while I'm around.'

Moss had been standing inconspicuously in the background, eyeing the woman with a wooden patience.

'Mrs Hodge' – hands in his pockets, he stayed where he was – 'why don't you shut up and let us get on with it? That way, you'll get rid of us in half the time.'

She gasped her indignation, eyes widening.

'Mum, please . . .' The girl made it an appeal.

The woman shrugged and fell silent.

'Let's start, Rose,' said Thane. 'Did Bootsy tell you who fixed that job for him with Durman Motors?'

'Fixed?' She frowned and moistened her lips. 'It wasn't fixed. Someone just told him about it, that's all.'

'A friend.' She ignored her mother's snort. 'I didn't meet the man but –' she stopped, frowning – 'I'm not sure but I think his name was Fraser. Bootsy called him something else.'

'You mean a nickname?' asked Thane, with a quick glance towards Moss.

She nodded. 'It was – yes, it was Iggy or Ziggy. Something like that.'

Thane restrained a whistle of satisfaction and quickly shaped his next question.

'How did Bootsy get along with Harry Durman?'

'All right, I suppose.' She shrugged, her mind still grappling with the basic need to accept what had happened. 'Why did they do it, mister? Why did they kill him?'

'Him – an' his boss last night,' muttered her mother from the background. 'Don't try to tell me there wasn't some crooked caper in all of it.'

Thane ignored the woman. 'Rose, all I know is that Bootsy asked me to meet him. He said it was important, but – well, he didn't get the chance to tell me what it was about.' He paused. 'Did he tell you much about his job? Was anything worrying him about it?'

Rose Hodge hesitated, then nodded. 'They made him work overtime – or Mr Durman did. It – he was angry about it.'

'Overtime?' Moss raised a surprised eyebrow. 'The showroom staff are moaning that business is dead.'

She winced at the word and answered wearily. 'All I know is he spent four nights at some special job – a private job, for a friend of Mr Durman's.' She turned to her mother for support. 'That's right, isn't it?'

'Or so he told us,' said Mrs Hodge bleakly. 'Wi' him, I wouldn't know if it was true.'

'But it was overtime and overtime usually means good money,' coaxed Thane patiently. 'Rose, should that make him angry?'

Again she hesitated, avoiding his gaze.

'Tell us and get it over with,' suggested Moss mildly. 'It's the easiest way.'

She sighed and nodded. 'He had to go to this place and repaint two vans as fast as he could – he wasn't told why or who the job was for and Mr Durman said he had to keep quiet about it. And – well, he was worried in case they were stolen, yet he said he had to do it in case he lost his job.' Her head came up and she looked earnestly at Thane. 'He was tryin' to go straight. He really was.'

'Nobody told your dad or me about this before,' said her mother grimly. 'We'd have had a thing or two to say, believe me.'

'I know – so did Bootsy,' countered the girl with a flash of spirit. 'You . . . you'd have blown a fuse. But it's true.'

'Did he tell you where he did this job?' asked Thane quietly.

'No.' She shook her head.

'Then did he say anything else about it? Anything at all?'

'Only the colour he was painting them. I remember that – it was dark blue. He had it on his hands for days afterwards.' Suddenly the memory seemed too much for her. She turned her head away and started to sob.

'Rose . . .' Crossing anxiously, Mrs Hodge put a quick, protective arm around her daughter's shoulders and glared defiantly at Thane. 'That's enough, mister – no more o' your questions. I mean it.'

'We're finished,' soothed Thane, while the girl continued to sob, her body shaking with emotion. 'You can tell her she helped – helped a lot.'

'Helped?' Mrs Hodge wasn't impressed. 'I jus' wish she'd never heard o' that damned ned Malloy.'

They made their own way out, closing the door behind them. Moss said nothing until they were at the foot of the stairway and heading towards the street. Then he gave a sudden, resonant belch, the sound magnified by the tunnel-like walls around.

'Two vans, painted dark blue – somebody's planning to have a fair-sized load to shift. Do we check the stolen list?'

Thane nodded, thinking of the girl they'd left. Rose – any kind of flower – would have a tough time surviving in these grimy tenements. If Bootsy Malloy had lived, if they'd eventually married, he wondered how it might have worked out.

But when they reached the street he was brought sharply back to the present. The two cars were as they'd left them, and Sergeant Francey Lang was standing at the kerb by the lead vehicle, the sunlight glinting on his tunic buttons and a hopeful grin on his face.

'Got a moment now, Mr Thane?' he asked as they reached him.

'All right,' surrendered Thane, ignoring Moss's grin. 'But keep it brief, Francey.'

'Brief as I can, sir,' agreed the community relations sergeant happily. 'If you still want Ziggy Fraser there's a damn good chance I can lay him on a plate for you – but it won't be till late tonight.'

Moss's grin faded while Thane stared at the man.

'You're sure?'

'Like I said, people around here owe me a few favours – and plenty of them hate Fraser's guts.' Sergeant Lang drooped one eyelid in a wink. 'So somebody I know is – ah – obliging.'

It was the best news Thane had heard all day. But Moss remained stubbornly sceptical.

'This contact – can you trust him?' he demanded, frowning.

'No.' Francey Lang rubbed his hands together blandly. 'But he knows I'll beat his ears off if he tries to fool me. The arrangement is I meet him again tonight, and he'll tell me then. The only thing is, I'll need to be alone, sir. He scares easily.'

'Meet him, but don't make a move after that on your own,' warned Thane. 'I mean that, Francey – no one man-band stuff.'

Lang nodded, ran a finger along the old razor scar on his face, and looked faintly embarrassed.

'There's something else, sir – the thing I tried to see you about earlier.'

'Well?' This time Thane felt prepared for anything.

'It's about Harry Durman. He went shopping for some warehouse space around Millside a few weeks back – said he needed sole occupancy, no questions asked, and that it had to be somewhere near the docks.' Lang paused and shrugged apologetically. 'He stopped asking after a spell, so it looks like he got fixed up. But nobody knows for sure.'

'Francey . . .' Moss swallowed then gave up. 'How the hell are we supposed to compete, Colin?'

'We don't even try.' Thane made a rapid revision of Francey Lang's worth. Electronic gear for a robbery, two vans for transport and a warehouse waiting – the men who'd now killed twice believed in fine detail planning. 'Francey, if you've anything else . . .'

'Not yet, sir.' Lang shook his head solemnly. 'But I'm trying.'

'Do that,' agreed Thane fervently. He glanced at his watch. 'Want a lift anywhere?'

'Well, maybe if you'd time, sir . . .' began Lang.

'Time?' Thane grinned. 'We'll do better than that. Inspector Moss is coming with me, so the other car and driver are spare. They're yours.'

Lang beamed, saluted, and was turning away when Thane stopped him.

'Francey, remember. When you hear about Ziggy Fraser all you do is contact me. Understood?'

'Aye.' Francey Lang nodded slowly, his eyes suddenly bleak. 'I know what he's like.'

Leaving them, he boarded the lead car. As it started up and pulled away, Phil Moss scraped one foot along the pavement and swore softly under his breath.

'Wandering around in a uniform and he comes up with almost as much as we've managed – where's the justice in it?' He sought solace in one of his stomach pills, swallowed it, then asked almost petulantly, 'Exactly where am I supposed to be going with you anyway?'

'Jarrold Walsh's club,' said Thane shortly.

Moss raised an eyebrow. 'Do we have a reason?'

'That depends on Walsh,' said Thane obliquely. 'Let's find out.'

Hope Street and Sauchiehall Street are respectively important among Glasgow's business and shopping arteries and the Silk Slipper Casino was neatly located on the top floor of a modern office building close to where they joined. Inside the ground-floor entrance hall a heavily built doorman had a silvered plastic sentry box shaped like a shoe. The rest of the décor was a rainbow array of synthetic silk drapes, each patterned with tiny silver slippers.

It was six p.m. and the height of the evening rush-hour for traffic when Thane walked in with Moss a couple of steps behind. Immediately, the doorman bobbed like a rabbit from his sentry box with a greeting which switched to a knowing lift of one eyebrow.

'Police?'

Thane nodded.

'Both of you?' The question, backed by doubt, was directed at Moss. Moss's tie-knot had sagged to a good two inches below a crumpled shirt-collar and his shoes looked like he'd been grave-digging.

'Both of us,' agreed Thane. 'Chief Inspector Thane – I'm looking for Jarrold Walsh.'

'Hold on.' The doorman disappeared into his plastic hideaway, they heard the ting of a telephone followed by a brief murmur, and in a matter of seconds he reappeared, looking happier.

'Mr Walsh says go straight up – he's waiting.'

A private elevator manned by another sample of hired muscle whisked them up to the top floor and they stepped out into the Silk Slipper's gaming area. It was too early for all the tables to be manned and the main custom in sight was a trio of elderly, well-dressed women who were feeding coins into a row of one-armed bandits.

'Reception committee,' murmured Moss suddenly, nudging Thane. Frank Walsh was coming towards them from the far end of the gaming area. 'Looks like we only rate the junior league welcome.'

Frank Walsh greeted them in friendly enough fashion then began guiding them through the gaming area towards his father's office suite.

'How long till things liven up?' asked Thane mildly, gesturing at the unlit tables around.

'From ten o'clock onward – but the real action is around midnight.' The younger man nodded a greeting to a pallid-faced croupier who was using a tiny whisk brush to dust a baccarat table. 'After that it goes on as long as their money and stamina last out.'

'Were you here last night?'

'I wondered when you'd ask.' Walsh was unperturbed. 'I stayed till about one a.m. If you feel you want confirmation just ask around. Either I was tackling paperwork in the office or I was out front giving the customers the happy smile treatment.'

'It helps to know,' murmured Thane.

Walsh grinned a little and nodded. They reached a frosted-glass door marked 'Private', went through into an outer office, and heard a murmur of voices coming from another room just ahead.

'Dad' – Frank Walsh led the way – 'here they are.'

'Makes you sound like the local garbage squad, Chief Inspector,' boomed Jarrold Walsh. In dinner jacket and black tie, the club owner was standing with a glass in his hand in the centre of the room. 'You've arrived in the middle of an unplanned family gathering.' He looked around, eyes twinkling a little behind their heavy spectacles. 'I – uh – gather you've already met Ruth and her brother.'

'That's right.' Thane nodded a greeting. 'Good to see you again, Miss Blantyre.'

Resplendent in a green velvet trouser suit, wearing diamond ear-rings almost as large as her engagement ring, Ruth Blantyre smiled up at him from the nearest of the big black leather armchairs in the room. Her brother stood behind her chair, leaning on it, an expression of unconcealed interest on his thin face. On the other side of the room, together on a couch, Tracy Walsh and Roy Davidson looked both nervous and uncomfortable and Thane had the feeling he and Moss had interrupted something by their arrival.

'Like a drink?' queried Jarrold Walsh. He nodded at the glass in his hand. 'I'm on gin, but name your choice.'

'Not now.' Thane shook his head and smiled.

'Moss?' Jarrold Walsh raised a hopeful eyebrow. 'You didn't tell me this morning you're another member of the ulcer club. I – ah – heard that when I was asking around later. But be like me. Try pickling the thing now and again.'

'Is it on the diet-sheet?' asked Moss incredulously.

'Is it hell. But it breaks the monotony. How about it?' He sighed as Moss shook his head. 'All right, what can I do for you both? You don't look like you're here to play the tables.'

'I wanted to clear up a couple of points.' Thane stopped and glanced around. 'But it might help if . . .'

'If it was just you and I?' The man nodded his understanding, drained his glass at a single gulp, and laid it on the desk. 'Right. No sense in everybody moving. We can go outside.'

'Dad . . .' Tracy Walsh stirred anxiously.

'Now don't you start next,' said her father firmly. 'I had enough of that from Frank this morning. Followed by you, Ruthy . . .'

'For your own good,' sighed Ruth Blantyre. 'I told you, Jarrold.'

'And you were right,' he admitted. Going over, he kissed her lightly, then stooped and picked up a fur jacket which had been lying on the floor. Draping it over the chair, he grinned at her. 'That's a damned expensive kind of foot-mat.'

Moss was nearest. He wandered a couple of steps nearer, considered the coat casually. 'Mink?' he asked.

'Correct,' answered Don Blantyre. He flicked the fur casually. 'You don't rate in the entertainment world till you've one in your wardrobe.'

'She had that coat when I met her,' agreed Jarrold Walsh sadly. 'I'm still trying to find out where it came from.'

'And you can keep guessing,' said Ruth Blantyre, then sighed. 'Jarrold, there's a chance Frank and Tracy could be right . . .'

'About having a lawyer?' Jarrold Walsh shook his head. 'Any other time but not now – this stays family.' He looked pointedly at Roy Davidson who'd been sitting quietly but listening. 'As much as it can, anyway.'

'Meaning me, Mr Walsh?' The long-haired young-ster flushed and reached for Tracy's hand. 'We've told you how things stand. And when it comes to Harry Durman's murder I've got problems too, remember?'

'That maybe goes for all of us until this is over,' mused Frank Walsh from the doorway. 'The chief inspector already wants to know what I was doing last night.'

'Why?' His father's bushy eyebrows formed large, surprised question-marks.

'Why not?' shrugged his son. 'It's no problem – right, Don?'

'I should know,' agreed Don Blantyre wryly. 'I was with him, Chief Inspector.'

'Here?'

The man nodded and grimaced wryly. 'Being the next best thing to family, I looked in for a free drink – and that got me landed in helping Frank sort out a damned mountain of paperwork. I didn't escape till after midnight.'

'As long as you kept your hand out of the till,' said Ruth Blantyre coldly. She glanced at Thane. 'Don told me about it happening, Chief Inspector – we've an apartment on the south side of town and he just got in ahead of me last night. But from his breath it wasn't just one drink.'

'For services rendered,' murmured her brother. 'Happy, Chief Inspector?'

Thane nodded.

'Then maybe we can have this talk you want,' grunted Jarrold Walsh.

'Good.' Thane glanced mildly towards Moss. 'Phil, tidy up those timings I talked about.'

'Might as well,' agreed Moss easily, reaching for his notebook. 'I won't take long.'

Leaving them, Thane followed Jarrold Walsh out of the room, through the outer office, and back out into the gaming area. Beckoning, Walsh guided him over to a softly lit painting on the wall near a roulette table. It was a reasonably good water-colour portrait of the club owner and he stopped beside it with pride.

'Like it?' he demanded.

'Yes, very much. Who painted it – Tracy?'

'Uh-huh.' Walsh's face creased with pleasure. 'She's got talent, Thane. In fact, anything to do with art and she's hooked.'

'Like this afternoon?' asked Thane quietly.

The man's face clouded. 'She told me what happened outside the Art Galleries. It didn't sound like an accident.'

'It wasn't. The man who was killed came from Durman's garage.'

Jarrold Walsh gave a soft whistle of apparently genuine surprise, and pushed his spectacles fractionally higher on his nose.

'And you were there . . .' He paused, eyes narrowing. 'Ruthy said you had a phone call when she was at your office, that it sounded like you were having to go out . . .'

Thane nodded, and Walsh gave a long sigh.

'Chief Inspector, it seems it's time we did talk – and seriously. What Ruthy told you was true. Durman did show up here a few days back – and I did throw him out on his ear.'

'Why did he come?' asked Thane neutrally. 'You seemed to make it pretty clear he wouldn't get the welcome mat.'

'That's true.' Walsh gave a grim, humourless chuckle. 'I walked in and found Durman in the outer office. He looked scared as a rabbit, then he started making noises about letting me in on some deal. But after the last time?' A snort underlined Walsh's reaction. 'He was lucky I heaved him out of the door and not through a window. But I didn't see him after that – or kill him, whatever some people may think.'

'Is that what's worrying Tracy and young Davidson?' asked Thane bluntly.

The man blinked, then laughed aloud. 'Hell, no! We're in the middle of a domestic drama, that's all. I blew up about how he should get his hair cut if he wanted me to like him hanging around Tracy so much.'

Thane smiled, looked at the portrait again, then

asked out of the blue, 'How long have you held a gaming licence?'

Jarrold Walsh's eyes narrowed instantly. 'Long enough to know the rules. You can see my register of members and tax returns – and ask the Gaming Board. I've a clean record.'

Thane nodded, knowing that otherwise the Silk Slipper wouldn't exist. The Government-sponsored Gaming Board was tough, with its own travelling inspectors who made unheralded spot checks on every club, checks which could include a fine detail survey of every item of gaming apparatus. One estimate was that gambling in Britain amounted to a £200 million a year industry from bingo onward, and the Gaming Board, created for that purpose, kept it tightly controlled.

'You've heard the saying "All men are gamblers" – and it's near enough to truth,' said Walsh softly, as if reading his mind. 'I've got one of my own. A wheel has no memory if you're giving a fair deal. Thane, this club is licensed, every man on my table staff is Board approved – I don't take chances of any kind.'

'That's what I heard,' murmured Thane. A roulette table not far away was coming to life with two gloomy-faced players facing an openly bored croupier. 'In fact, the way it came to me was more of a warning.'

Chuckling, Jarrold Walsh led the way back to his office. Moss was at the window, looking out, and the others were sitting around, waiting patiently.

'Finished, Phil?' asked Thane.

'All we need,' answered Moss easily.

Leaving the window, he weaved his way through the chairs towards Thane. Then, halfway over, he suddenly stumbled, started to fall, and grabbed at Ruth Blantyre's chair for support, almost landing in her lap. Steadying himself, he got up with a mutter of apology.

'It's the carpet,' declared Don Blantyre sardonically. 'Jarrold fixes trip-wires in it to foil irate punters after his blood. Speaking as a potential brother-in-law . . .'

'Not now, Don,' frowned Jarrold Walsh, cutting him short. 'Are you all right, Moss?'

'Fine.' Moss rubbed his chin and looked around. 'Sorry – I stubbed my toe on one of these chairs. Thanks, Miss Blantyre.'

Ruth Blantyre raised an eyebrow. 'I'm not sure why, but it was a pleasure.'

Moss grinned sheepishly. Then, like Thane, he said goodbye and they left.

It was still rush-hour time outside the Silk Slipper and a traffic snarl-up stretched in both directions along the street. Horns were hooting and the air was thick with exhaust fumes as they walked along to the Millside car.

'That was a pretty interesting fall,' said Thane, straight-faced. 'With a soft landing – how did you make out?'

'Pretty good.' Moss winked at him, and held out his hand with the fingers clutching a small tuft of champagne-coloured hairs. 'Best mink – that's what you wanted, wasn't it?'

Thane nodded appreciatively. 'We'll try them on Dan Laurence.'

'And if they happen to match the ones from Harry Durman's car?' queried Moss, stopping at the Millside car and reaching for the door handle.

'Then we've really got something to stir up,' said Thane grimly.

A mink coat and two murders. For an odd reason

he couldn't pin down he hoped he'd be wrong. But if the Scientific Bureau's comparison microscopes came up with a positive result then Ruth Blantyre was going to need more than her full-bloom looks and personality to ease out of some awkward, non-social questioning.

Chapter Five

The worst time for any cop is when he is waiting, knowing the lid is ready to burst off but with no idea when or where. Colin Thane had gone through it before and expected he would again, plenty of times. But that didn't make it any easier – and at Millside Division things showed every sign of shaping into a long, long night.

By nine p.m., when dusk came round, he was no further forward. Outside, the city's streets were dry and windy and the overnight weather forecast was set for fair. The early editions of the next day's morning papers were already out, with Harry Durman's death relegated to a few inches on an inside page and Bootsy Malloy's killing viewed as just one more hit-and-run street fatality. Even if some burrowing crime reporter had managed to link the two it would hardly have mattered – the Scotland–Holland game now ruled supreme, from stories of the first Dutch fans arriving in an armada of charter flights to pull-out picture souvenirs of the teams and long columns of analysis and forecasts by every sports writer who wasn't too far gone on tranquillizers.

'While here we sit like birds in the flaming wilderness,' grumbled Phil Moss sourly. Slouched in a chair, his feet propped on Thane's desk, he scowled at the Divisional crime map. 'And where will it get us?'

Thane shrugged. He felt more like a crow on a

telegraph pole but he knew exactly what Moss meant – and the reason lay in front of him, a typed operational order from Headquarters signed by Buddha Ilford.

'Read it again,' he invited, flicking the sheet across the desk.

'Why?' Moss used a heel to shove it back again. 'If that's the best Headquarters can do . . .' His stomach rumbled a loud and adequate conclusion.

Repeated for every division in the city, probably duplicated by county forces in the surrounding areas, it amounted to a maximum surveillance plan. Millside Division's share was six specified locations with electronic security apparatus and, by Ilford's reckoning, a high risk situation. All to be put under special watch and guard.

Night-shift men had been brought in early, day-shift men had been held on duty. Divisional resources had been drained – and the remnant of men left to maintain regular routine were only praying that the rest of the world would decide on a quiet night.

'Once it happens . . .' began Thane.

'If it happens,' grunted Moss. 'Suppose it doesn't.'

'Then there's tomorrow – and the next day,' answered Thane wearily. 'Or maybe Francey Lang.' He glanced at his wrist-watch, wondering how much longer it would be before they heard from the community involvement sergeant. 'But otherwise Buddha has it spelled out – we wait.'

Moss muttered a comment on Ilford's general ancestry. 'So we wait here on our backsides?'

'On our backsides,' confirmed Thane wryly. 'Look, Phil, I'm the character that's supposed to be low on patience around here. Let's keep it that way – anyway, what's left to do?'

Slouching deeper into his chair, Moss shrugged. 'The Walsh girl is worried – and boy-friend looks scared. We could light some kind of fire under them and find out why they don't like us.'

'Because they don't like us?' Thane raised an eyebrow. 'Start that and you'll end up with half the population sharing the same bonfire.' He lit another cigarette, heard a telephone ring in the main office, and paused. But the call wasn't switched through. 'All right, Jarrold Walsh and his family keep popping up in the damnedest ways – but they've still a family-sized alibi around them.'

'Hand-sewn,' muttered Moss.

Thane nodded. He had the remains of a scribbling pad in front of him, the top sheet covered with doodled names and one-word queries. It was the end product of two hours' joint effort – and it meant nothing.

'There are fire escapes at the Silk Slipper . . .' began Moss.

'We went over that. Like we timetabled Davidson and the Walsh girl – and Jarrold Walsh with the Blantyre woman,' said Thane wearily.

Allow for lying and none of them could be completely ruled out. Allow for an unknown motive and . . . He shook his head, gave up, then grabbed eagerly for the telephone as it suddenly rang.

'Thane . . .'

'Dan Laurence.' The Scientific Bureau chief's voice came over the line with a relaxed good humour behind it. 'Got Phil Moss with you, Colin?'

'Yes, he's here.' Thane mouthed Laurence's name to Moss, who swung his feet down and quickly sat upright.

'Well now, you can give him many thanks for his latest little offering,' rumbled Laurence, then released a chuckle. 'Mink, he said, right?'

'That's why we gave you it,' answered Thane,

frowning. 'Dan, those hairs you found in Durman's car . . .'

'Were mink, laddy.' The Scientific Bureau chief gave a mock sigh. 'Tell Moss the lady he knows goes in for high-grade rabbit . . .'

'Rabbit?' Thane swallowed. 'Now look, Dan . . .'

'Rabbit,' said Laurence positively. 'It happens, Colin. Tarted-up bunny – you can get away with it if you know the right furrier.'

'And if you've the mink image.' Thane glanced across at Moss and saw his gloom reflected in the other's scrawny features. 'So that's it?'

'That's it,' confirmed Laurence. 'Eh . . . still, I can help you a wee bit in another direction. That story you got from Bootsy Malloy's girl about him respraying a couple o' vans. Dark blue she said, right?'

'Yes.'

'She's right. One o' my lads checked the overalls Malloy was wearin' – positive traces of dark blue, and we double-checked the Durman Motors paint stock. They've nothing there that matches.'

'It's better than nothing,' agreed Thane. 'Thanks, Dan.'

He said goodbye and hung up with a grimace.

'Like birds in the wilderness,' said Moss greyly.

Thane nodded. 'You in your wilderness, me on my telegraph pole.'

And a TV actress who built her mink-lined reputation on rabbit-skins . . . yes, it was going to be a long night.

Buddha Ilford telephoned at nine-thirty, a short, curt call mainly aimed at letting them know he was still at Headquarters. But he'd heard about the rabbit-hairs.

'I happen to have assigned this operation the

codename "Mink",' he said caustically. 'Well, we've clattered down the social scale, agreed?'

'Operation Bunny-Rabbit, sir,' answered Thane, grimacing at the receiver. 'I'm sorry. We thought . . .'

'Thought wrong, snapped Ilford impatiently. 'Thane, when I heard about this alleged mink I had Central Division put a couple of men on this woman's tail . . . just in case you were right. That's finished.'

'Yes, sir.' There was nothing else he could say.

'Right.' Ilford's disgust was no longer concealed. 'I'll be here. Stay in touch.'

The distant receiver slammed down. Sadly, Thane replaced his own.

'Operation Bunny-Rabbit.' Moss glared at him balefully. 'Always the ruddy diplomat, aren't you?' Then, slowly, the glare died and he began to chuckle softly. 'But I wish I'd seen Buddha's face when he was told.'

Thane could imagine the moment. And was glad he hadn't been around.

Time dragged by while the night-team sergeant dealt with the Division's quota of after-dark crime and the men on what all Millside now called Operation Bunny-Rabbit idled around, smoked too much, and waited.

Phil Moss settled for his own amusement, flicking paper-clips at a home-made target on top of Thane's office filing cabinet. His aim had improved to five out of six hits at six feet before the telephone rang again.

He got to it first, grunted an answer, then swiftly passed over the receiver. 'Francey Lang . . .'

106

'Where are you, Francey?' demanded Thane.

'Fidra Street, sir – near the old West Quayside.' Lang's voice was low and unusually excited.

'Fidra Street.' Thane glanced at Moss who nodded and crossed to the wall-map. 'Right, Francey, we've got it. What about Ziggy Fraser?'

'He's here,' confirmed Lang. The community involvement sergeant broke off and Thane heard a faint muttering at the other end of the line.

'Francey?'

'Sorry, sir.' Lang gave a hoarse chuckle. 'A – well, a friend of mine just decided to leave, and quickly. Fraser's here all right – I saw him two minutes back.'

Thane tensed. 'Right, Francey. Hold on.' He slipped a hand over the mouthpiece. 'He's located him, Phil – get a couple of cars out front.'

'Right.' Moss bounded for the intercom. As he pressed the switch and began speaking, Thane turned his attention back to the telephone.

'We're coming out now, Francey. Where do we meet you?'

For a moment he heard only Lang's heavy breathing on the line then the man made up his mind.

'Best place will be the West Quayside end of Fidra Street, sir. I'm near there now, at a public call box. Fraser's at a scrap-dealer's yard about five hundred yards north of me.'

'Alone?'

'When I saw him, sir. But I can't be sure.'

'Then stay put till we get there.' Grinning, Thane hung up and saw Moss waiting. 'We've got him, Phil. You and I go in from the West Quayside end. The other car takes the north end – but doesn't move till ordered.'

'I'm ready,' said Moss happily. 'Erickson's driving –
so let's go.'

Under ten minutes took them from the centre of Millside to the dimly lit streets around dockland and as
the old West Quayside loomed up Thane ordered
Erickson to slow. Engine a whisper, the police Jaguar
crawled past the gaunt, black quayside wharves
towards the start of Fidra Street and in another
moment they saw the telephone box, a bright island
of light against a featureless background of warehouse buildings.

But the telephone box was empty.

'Where the hell is Francey?' muttered Moss, frowning round.

'Damn him, he was told not to move.' Thane
gnawed his lip while the radio began crackling, a
message that the back-up car was in position at the
north end of the street. 'Pull in, Erickson.'

The car swung to halt at the kerb beside the empty
telephone box. The radio was crackling again,
requesting an acknowledgement, but Thane ignored
it, straining his eyes against the shadowed gloom of
the empty street, his earlier confidence evaporating.
Then, as he made up his mind and reached for the
door handle, a flurry of movement erupted into
the roadway halfway along Fidra Street.

'Sir . . .' Erickson gave a warning grunt.

'Lights,' snapped Thane harshly.

The Jaguar's long-range halogen lamps lanced white
through the night as Erickson slapped their switches.
At the same time, without waiting for orders, he
flicked into gear and rammed the accelerator.

On ahead, and bathed in the white light, half a
dozen figures had their quarry on the ground and
were booting him. Startled, they didn't move for a

moment while the Jaguar roared towards them. Then, reacting, they tried to scatter. But Erickson twisted the wheel, swung it hard over again, and brought the car to a squealing halt which blocked their path.

First out as the car doors flew open, Thane dived for the nearest ned while a knife slashed for his face. He ducked the blade, slammed his elbow up hard into the man's mouth, and followed it with a coldly calculated knee into the man's groin. Yowling in agony, the ned slumped back as Thane swung round ready for the next one.

Beside the car, Erickson's bulky figure was in baton-swinging action against two attackers. To his right, Phil Moss had tackled a ned who looked twice his size – and at that precise moment sent him sprawling with a fast-moving judo grip.

'Phil – on your left . . .' Thane yelled the warning as another thug in an old army combat jacket sprang at Moss, swinging an iron bar. Then he had troubles of his own again as a swearing, slobbering shape came straight for him with a similar weapon.

Grappling the man, Thane took a glancing blow from the bar on his shoulder, winced at the pain, but managed to seize the ned's wrist before he could swing again. Spinning him round, Thane caught the reek of the man's beer-fumed breath, then used one of gangland's own vicious tricks – a head-butt which took the ned squarely on the nose and brought a crunching of bone and cartilege.

The iron bar dropped and forgotten, the man screamed and tore himself free, hands going up to his face as he staggered blindly.

And Thane found himself faced by two more. Framed in the white headlamp beams, one was Ziggy Fraser and the other a brute-faced 'heavy', neither of them so far committed to the brawl.

A small man but hawk-featured, Fraser was in

109

slacks amd a tailored sports coat which buttoned up to the neck. For a moment he stared at Thane, eyes glittering, then he gave a soft command to the 'heavy' at his side.

A 'heavy' with a gun. Thane saw the muzzle come up, threw himself clear as it barked, and heard glass shatter somewhere behind him. A second shot slammed out while he hit the ground in a frantic roll towards the Jaguar and cover.

Then there was a new sound, the roar of a high-revving engine as the other Millside car arrived. It squealed to a halt, the crew came tumbling out, and their eruption on the scene was a signal for the remaining neds to scatter. Scrambling upright, ready to shout a warning about the gun, Thane swore instead. Ziggy Fraser and his minder had already vanished into the darkness.

His shoulder aching where the iron bar had grazed it, Thane looked round. Erickson had one ned draped groaning over the Jaguar's radiator grille and another was being briskly frisked and handcuffed by two of the newly arrived Millside D.C.s. But the others had gone – and Phil Moss was bending over an all-too-familiar figure lying in the middle of the roadway.

Francey Lang had been wearing a light civilian raincoat over his uniform. Now it was ripped to rags down one side and was heavily bloodstained. He lay on the grimy tarmac with legs still drawn up pro-tectively against his body, arms covering his head, and a faint, coarse, whistling noise coming from his battered lips every time he breathed.

'Damn them all.' Looking up as Thane arrived, Moss swore with a deep-felt pungency. 'How many did you count, Colin?'

'Two we got, maybe another half-dozen we didn't. Fraser got away.' Grim-faced, Thane noted the starred glass round a bullet-hole in the Jaguar's windshield,

110

then beckoned the nearest plain-clothes man. The man came over. His name was Hudson, he was young, but he took one glance at Francey Lang and suddenly looked much older and harder.

'Radio control,' said Thane wearily. 'We need an ambulance.'

'Yes, sir.' Hudson thumbed bleakly towards the blackness of the surrounding alleys. 'We could go after the others and . . .'

'Don't be a damned fool,' said Moss wearily, joining them. He had taken off his coat to pillow Francey Lang's head. 'They'll be well away by now, laddy.'

'And one's got a shooter,' concluded Thane. He shook his head. 'Mop up what we have.'

'Yes, sir.' Hudson was disappointed but turned away.

The only man who still looked mildly happy was Erickson. He came padding over with a gash on his forehead which gave his Viking features an almost satanic aspect, reached them, and grimaced.

'Not much of a fight, sir.'

'You got one of yours,' said Thane. 'We can use him.'

'He didn't do my baton any good.' Erickson considered the Jaguar's bullet-smashed windshield for the first time and looked more thoughtful. 'Still, it could have been worse, I suppose. How about Sergeant Lang?'

'We'll let the hospital decide,' said Thane almost curtly. The job wasn't over. 'Get a torch from the car. We've work to do.'

Erickson nodded, returned in a moment with the torch, and followed Thane along Fidra Street to the scrapyard.

'Sir?' Erickson raised an eyebrow as they stopped at the locked door.

Thane nodded and the driver's large, booted foot

111

swung once. His heel took the wood of the door just below the lock with scientific accuracy and a loud splintering, and a second pile-driving kick was sufficient to send the door swinging open.

They went in and Erickson played the hand-torch beam around. Mounds of haphazardly piled junk met the light, from rusted metal scrap to salvaged timber. But the whole yard had a dank, disused appearance and the only sign of life was the quick, scurrying sound of tiny feet and here and there a bright glint of tiny, watching eyes.

'Lousy with rats,' grunted Erickson. 'How about the office, sir?'

'Not yet.' Thane took the torch from him and used the beam at close quarters on a crumpled length of oddly stained tarpaulin lying near. The stains were dark blue, misting at the edges and dry to the touch. When he swung the beam away, he spotted an old paint can on its side near some timber. Going over, he saw traces of the same dark blue paint inside. Satisfied, he thumbed towards the office hut. 'We'll try it now.'

Another kick forced the hut door, Erickson found a switch inside, and a single, naked electric bulb lit the shabby interior. A single table and a couple of chairs were the only furnishings, and a clock on the wall looked as though it hadn't worked in years. But the place had been used, and recently. The rough wooden floor was littered with cigarette stubs.

'Sir . . .' Erickson stooped beside the table and pointed. Several small ends of electrical wiring lay on the floor beside blobs of hardened solder.

Thane nodded. The next stage was for the Scientific Branch and a fingerprint squad. But it didn't need an expert to spell out what they'd found. Bootsy Malloy had come here to respray those two mysterious vans. Harry Durman might have been another visitor and certainly someone had worked on electrical apparatus.

Except that whatever the scrapyard had been used for its role had been almost over.

They went back to the cars. An ambulance had arrived and Francey Lang was being loaded aboard on a stretcher. The ned who had been batoned by Erickson was pushed after him in handcuffs with a plain-clothes man as escort, then the ambulance growled off with its blue emergency light flashing.

Thane left the rest of the C.I.D. car's crew to guard the scrapyard. When he returned to the Jaguar their other captive, also handcuffed, was in the rear seat with Moss. He climbed in beside them, nodded to Erickson, and they started back towards Millside.

The ned between them was sullen, dry-lipped and silent. He looked about twenty, he was thin with lank, greasy hair, and wore the standard uniform of his kind – a studded leather jacket, sweat shirt, blue jeans and heavy boots. From his breath he's been drinking and from the way he nursed his stomach he'd been hit where it hurt.

'What's your name?' demanded Moss suddenly.

'Get stuffed,' said the ned bitterly.

'That's a nice name,' said Moss, unperturbed. 'Suits you, laddy.'

The ned turned and spat. Moss considered the white globule of spittle on his jacket then, expression unchanged, grabbed him by the hair and rubbed the ned's face against the spot.

'We asked your name,' he said softly. 'Don't strain my patience – I'm not the kind.'

Swallowing, their captive glanced at Thane. 'I – I didn't do anythin' . . .'

'Name,' said Thane bleakly. 'When it comes to attempted murder I like to know who I'm charging.'

'Mister –' the ned's eyes widened – 'now look . . .'

113

'Attempted murder as a starter,' snarled Thane, with little need to over-act. 'That's for Sergeant Lang. But there's Bootsy Malloy – and Harry Durman. Don't forget them.'

'Not wi' me.' The sullenness gave way to open panic. 'I was wi' Ziggy Fraser, right. But only tonight . . .'

'We didn't ask,' said Moss wearily. 'Just your name.'

'Joe – Joe Rogan.' The handcuffs chinked as Rogan tried to gesture his anxiety. 'Look, I'm tellin' it for real – maybe I thumped your sergeant a couple o' times, like everybody was doin'. But that's all.'

The Jaguar stopped briefly at traffic lights, then purred away again as they changed to green. A cinema was emptying on the corner, its audience scattering to parked cars or to queue at bus stops.

'Mister, I'm not carryin' any loads for Ziggy,' tried Rogan again. He licked his lips. 'I got this word, see, an' . . .'

Thane cut him short. 'Caution him, Phil.'

Quickly, Moss muttered his way through the formal caution. Up front, eyes on the road, Erickson listened with a mild interest.

'Now,' invited Thane as the caution finished. 'What word – and when?'

'A couple o' weeks back, that Ziggy had a job lined up an' was hirin' – you know how it goes.' Rogan looked at them earnestly. 'So – well, I said I was interested, like. An' then I met Ziggy to fix it up. But I haven't seen him since, so help me. Not till tonight . . .'

'When's the job?' asked Thane softly.

The ned shook his head. 'Any time now, accordin' to Ziggy. But don't ask me where, mister – I don't know. Just that he needs about a dozen o' us for it, an' there's two thousand quid a head for us when it's done.'

114

Moss whistled softly while Thane did some fast arithmetic. At that kind of pay-scale for the hired muscle the job had to be big, very big.

'You're trying to tell us you signed on blind?' asked Moss sceptically. He took Rogan's nod with a snort, then demanded, 'Then what was tonight's caper about?'

For a moment Rogan didn't answer and avoided their gaze. Then he shrugged. 'Ziggy was just makin' sure . . .'

'That you knew about Bootsy Malloy?' queried Thane sharply.

The ned nodded silently, looked down at the handcuffs, then blurted, 'If that damned cop o' yours hadn't shown up as we were leavin' . . .' He stopped, swallowed again, then shook his head despairingly. 'Hell, what did he expect Ziggy to do – play footsy wi' him?'

'All right,' said Thane softly. 'The charge stays attempted murder for now, Rogan – and God help you if you're lying.'

'I'm not.' Rogan drew a deep breath. 'You'll find out, mister – believe me.'

'We'll want names,' mused Moss.

'I said Ziggy . . .'

'The others,' said Thane grimly. 'All of them.'

Slowly, unhappily, Rogan shook his head. 'Mister, you know about Ziggy. The word's been out you want him. But that's my lot – my mates are my mates.'

'And they'd carve your ears off for starters if you talked?' Thane knew that, for the time being at any rate, the ned meant it. 'But Ziggy isn't running the show, is he?'

'No.' Rogan felt on safer ground. 'He says it's a contract job, all laid on. We get the stuff, the character who dreamed up the job pays out – but that's all he told us.' He tried a feeble grin. 'That's straight, mister. Wait an' you'll see.'

The uniformed staff at Millside police station processed Joe Rogan in a matter of minutes from formally charging him to searching his pockets then escorting him off towards the cells. As he was marched off, Thane used the desk sergeant's telephone, checked with Ambulance Control that Francey Lang had been taken to the Western Infirmary, and tried there next.

The Western's casualty officer was polite but firm. Sergeant Lang was undergoing emergency surgery and it was going to be another hour before any kind of medical report would be issued.

'But you can collect your prisoner any time,' added the Casualty officer acidly. 'Sooner the better, Chief Inspector. Only next time you send that kind of customer give me warning and I'll take pictures for the medical journals – what happened to him?'

'He tripped and fell,' said Thane woodenly. 'Thanks, Doctor.' Hanging up, he met the charge sergeant's gaze and shrugged. 'Too early to say about Francey. Can you get his wife over there?'

The man nodded. 'I'll fix it, sir. No problems.'

'Good.' He looked round for Moss, saw him at the far end of the room, and waved him over. 'Phil, our other ned's ready for collection.'

'Meaning I've to do it?' Moss sighed acceptance. 'What about you?'

'Buddha Ilford first – I'll go and talk to him.' Thane grimaced at the prospect. 'Then maybe I'll look in on Francey.'

Moss nodded a silent understanding, glanced at the clock on the wall, sighed again, and headed out.

The Headquarters interview wasn't as bad as it might have been, partly because Buddha Ilford was tired – late-night vigils took him harder than they had a few years back. The city C.I.D. chief had already heard some of it and listened grimly to the rest. Then, at the finish, he made his decisions with a scowling efficiency.

'All right, we call off the watch details for tonight. But they'll stand every night from now on – and I don't want to hear any moaning. This thug with the gun was Fraser's personal minder?'

Thane nodded. 'It looked that way, sir.'

'I don't want to start arming men wholesale.' Ilford spent a moment or two thinking about it. 'That can wait. But we'll do it if necessary.'

'Yes, sir.' When neds used guns, an armed cop made more sense than having to award somebody a posthumous medal. But Thane knew Ilford still loathed the idea. 'I'd like something else done.'

'Well?' Ilford raised an eyebrow.

'A twenty-four-hour surveillance on the Walsh family, sir.'

'You mean the whole damned tribe?' Ilford stared at him in dismay, then slowly shook his head. 'Can't be done. We haven't the men – not for that on top of everything else!'

'Then Jarrold Walsh on his own,' temporized Thane.

Ilford sighed. 'You don't give up, do you?' Picking up his pipe, he used a thumbnail to scrape the bowl. 'All right, we'll manage that. Anything more?'

Thane shook his head.

'Thank God for that,' said Ilford gravely. 'We're

117

about down to the canteen staff – and the way they cook, I wouldn't gamble whose side they're on.'

It was after midnight when Thane reached the Western Infirmary, entering the brightly lit casualty section behind a trolley which carried a road accident victim. She was a girl of about twenty, unconscious and bloody, and the casualty staff ignored him as they got to work.

Turning away, he suddenly saw Phil Moss coming towards him from the inquiry desk. Moss had a slim, pale-faced woman with him. She had dark hair, wore a white belted raincoat, and forced a smile as they reached him.

'Francey's wife, Colin,' introduced Moss, then grinned at her encouragingly. 'She's seen him and he's shaping up all right – one of the benefits of having a thick head.'

'He was lucky – or so the doctors say.' She spoke quietly, keeping control of her voice with an effort. 'Well, it isn't the first time. But I'd thought – with this new job . . .'

Thane nodded his understanding. 'Maybe you should go home now, Mrs Lang. We can give you a car.'

'No.' She shook her head firmly. 'I'll stay for a spell. The hospital people don't mind. I – well, I'd like to be here. Just in case.'

'We'll fix something.' Moss turned away, stopped a passing nurse, and spoke to her briefly. The nurse nodded and came over, smiling.

'I'll find you a cup of tea, Mrs Lang,' she suggested, and guided her away.

'I'd settle for something stronger.' Thane was relieved Francey's wife had gone. It didn't pay to think of cops as people with families or you ended up thinking of your own. 'Is he conscious?'

Moss nodded. 'And we can have a couple of minutes – official. But you can forget that ned I collected. Same story as Rogan except he's howling about police brutality. I took him back and booked him. Doc Williams will look at him later, just in case.'

That was routine too. Damaged neds could make their own kind of trouble if they found the right lawyer and a sympathetic jury.

Francey Lang was in a ward on the second floor. The night sister on duty, a fair-haired girl who looked as though she should still have been at school, frowned a little as she saw them.

'Two minutes and no more,' she reminded firmly. 'And you wouldn't get that much if it was up to me.'

'It'll be enough,' Thane assured her. 'How is he?'

'All right for the moment. They'll try and do more for him in the morning – he's to be in theatre again at nine. There's some pain, but we've given him something and he'll be sleeping soon.' She pursed her lips. 'Two minutes.'

She led them to a side room. Francey Lang lay motionless in a hospital cot, his face swollen and bruised against the white of the sheets, one eye half-shut. But the other eye flicked open and he mumbled a greeting as Thane bent over him.

'We got two of them, Francey,' said Thane quietly.

'Ziggy Fraser?' asked Lang in a hoarse whisper.

'No.' Thane saw the man's disappointment and heard a sound like a sigh coming from the battered lips. 'What happened, Francey?'

'They – they were starting to leave. I – I saw Fraser going an' tried to follow him.' Lang made a weak noise of disgust. 'But I made a – a right mess of it. Thanks for getting me out before they . . .'

'Thank Erickson,' interjected Moss gruffly. 'He thinks he'll need a new baton.'

'Tell the big ape I – I'll buy him a gold-plated one.' Lang tried to grin but it ended as a wince. 'Looks like I'll miss tomorrow's game. Still – maybe it wasn't a complete foul-up.' His words were beginning to slur but he kept on doggedly. 'That big minder Fraser had along . . .'

'The one with the shooter,' nodded Thane. 'What about him, Francey?'

'He – he said something to Fraser when they grabbed me, before I tried to get away' – Lang's good eye closed briefly then he forced it open with an effort – 'something about how they could use another uniform.'

'And Fraser?' Thane bent closer, ignoring a throat-clearing protest from the night sister, who was hovering near. 'What did he say, Francey?'

'Just that – that they'd got enough. Then they started – they started on me.'

'Thanks, Francey.' Thane stood back. 'Don't worry about things, here or at home.'

Lang mumbled vaguely and nodded. Lips pursed, the night sister signalled them to leave.

Outside in the corridor she made her feelings plain. 'He wasn't fit for that. Not in the state he's in. You – you're his own kind. You should have known better.'

'Damn it, woman,' grumbled Moss. 'He's a cop – he knew we'd come.'

Thane eased between them. 'How bad was it?' he asked quietly.

'As bad as I've seen.' Her expression made it plain she'd ample experience. 'The preliminary report is broken ribs, a fractured left arm and major bruising over the stomach and kidneys – plus what you saw. It'll need a consultant in the morning before we're sure of the internal picture. But if he'd taken much more he'd have died.'

When they left the hospital the city lay spread like a fairyland twinkle of lights under the night sky and the light wind blew fresh and clean. Upwards of a million people were out there, most of them asleep, most of them law-abiding citizens who thought of cops in terms of parking tickets if they thought of them at all.

Colin Thane looked up at the second floor, where the casualty ward's lights contributed their own soft glow. Then he turned towards the city again, his mind filled with a cold, bitter anger. Beside him, Phil Moss gave a long, muted belch and followed it with a yawn.

'There's tomorrow,' said Moss. 'And damn all we can do till then anyway.'

Thane nodded and they walked over to their car.

Chapter Six

Colin Thane slept at home that night. But the house felt strangely empty without Mary and the kids, felt different in a way he didn't like, and he slept badly. Finally he got up about seven a.m., and was in the kitchen burning toast and brewing coffee when a clatter at the letter-box announced the arrival of the morning's mail.

There were two bills and a postcard from Mary. He tossed the bills into a drawer where he could forget them till the end of the month and grinned as he read the scrawl on the postcard.

'Everything fine except for midges, and the cottage is a dream. Kids say wish you were here – so do I. Love, Mary.'

The picture on the front showed an impossibly colourful sunset against a background of hills and heather. He propped the postcard against the milk bottle while he ate and was finishing when the doorbell rang.

It was Phil Moss. He followed Thane back to the kitchen, found himself another cup without invitation, and gave a gargantuan yawn while he helped himself to the last of the coffee.

'You're early on the road.' Thane caught the cigarette Moss tossed him, lit it, and sat back. 'That landlady throw you out?'

'The next best thing.' Moss tasted his coffee,

grimaced, and reached for the sugar again. 'The idiot woman rented a couple of spare rooms to a mad horde of Dutch football fans, and they had a party most of the night.' The memory made him sigh. 'Red-currant gin and folk dances – wild men. I gave up and went back to the office. At least I got my head down there for a spell, which was better than nothing.'

Thane grinned. The same thing was probably happening in several homes.

'Any word about Francey Lang?' he asked.

'Doing all right, so far.' Moss paused for a minor belch. 'We're getting regular reports from the hospital. One of the nurses knows him.'

'Somebody everywhere knows Francey,' mused Thane dryly. The thought triggered another. 'Any sign of our two neds wanting to do more talking?'

Moss shook his head. 'The other way round. They've clammed up tight now – and they're scared they've said too much already. And before you ask, there's not as much as a sniff of Ziggy Fraser. He's vanished like he was some kind of mole.'

Anything else would have surprised Thane. A ned like Fraser always operated against a background of 'safe' houses and bought contacts which made disappearing an easy matter. But there was some consolation in the way they'd scattered his hired help. Getting them together again or finding replacements might take time.

'His boss won't be too happy,' murmured Moss, echoing his thoughts.

Thane nodded. 'Either they decide they'll postpone the whole deal till things cool down or . . .'

'Or they'll go in fast,' finished Moss. 'Right, so what do we do?'

'Keep looking – and hoping.' Thane put the milk bottle back in the refrigerator, dumped the coffee cups and dishes in the sink to wash another time, and frowned at them. 'We need another try at this, Phil. From as far back as we can go.'

'The bingo hall fire, you mean?' Moss made a rebellious grimace. 'The arson squad say we're wasting our time on that.'

'Maybe they were looking for something different.' Thane collected a fresh packet of cigarettes from a cupboard and reached for his jacket. 'Try it again, Phil.'

Moss gave a gloomy nod. 'What else, master?'

'Anything that grows from them. I've a problem of my own to sort that goes back in time – remembering where I met Jarrold Walsh before.'

'If it mattered would he have talked about it?' asked Moss sceptically.

'He might. Either way, it niggles me.' Pulling on his jacket, Thane took a last look around the kitchen, ready to leave. 'Right now, anything to do with the Walsh clan interests me.'

'On a wild hunch,' snorted Moss, then modified it. 'All right, I feel that way too. But it's no help.'

Thane nodded wryly. 'I know. But if we're right then by now they know we're chasing Ziggy Fraser – only they can't be sure why and our job is to keep them guessing. As long as it stays that way . . .'

'Someone might get careless?' Moss accepted the possibility with minimal enthusiasm. 'Mind telling me what you'll be doing while I'm getting dust in my throat in that file-room?'

'Starting from the beginning again, at Francey's exhibition hall.' Thane led the way towards the door. 'Second time round, things may look different.'

Two hours later he wasn't so sure. At the King Street hall, where part of the Project Community exhibition had been dismantled, the little caretaker positively scurried to show him around. But he drew a blank, and it was the same at Durman's apartment. From there he went to the Durman Motors showroom – to find only the office girl had bothered to come in for work. The rest of the staff had gone job-hunting.

Columba Street was next on his list. There, at least, the beginning was better. Rose Hodge was at home and her mother had gone out shopping. Wearing a black sweater and skirt, Bootsy Malloy's girl greeted him wearily and took him through to the kitchen.

'More questions?' she asked, gesturing him towards a chair.

'A few.' Thane sat down and waited while she took another chair opposite.

'Just be finished before my mum gets back.' She sounded composed, though her eyes were still red and swollen. 'Her and my dad – they mean well, but they never thought much of Bootsy. Now it's worse. So you'd better keep it short.'

Thane nodded agreement. One brush with Mrs Hodge had been enough to last him a long time.

'Just tell me about Bootsy. Things you did, places you went.'

'But –' she chewed her lip, disliking the idea – 'well, will it help?'

'It might. Try it, Rose. Even if it hurts a little.'

Her small shoulders shrugged beneath the cheap black sweater. 'If that's what you want.'

From there she still needed coaxing. But after a minute or so the girl seemed to find it easier and soon the story was tumbling out – from how she'd first met the fair-haired ned to the battles she'd had when her family had learned a little about Malloy's background.

Making an occasional, encouraging noise, Thane listened while she went on. A tap was dripping over at the kitchen sink and he could hear the muffled yowl of a radio coming through the wall from the house next door. Most of what Rose Hodge was saying didn't matter and he caught himself sniffing the faint, slum smell of bad drains and wondering when a sanitary inspector had last been round.

Then, suddenly, she made him jerk upright.

'Start that bit again,' he said quickly. 'From the beginning, Rose.'

She blinked. 'All I said was that the last time I went out with Bootsy it was raining an' he hadn't any money . . .'

'Right. And he took you where?'

'He – we went along to the Kelvingrove Art Galleries.' The girl shrugged again. 'It was his idea, but plenty of people do that when it's raining.'

Thane raised an eyebrow. 'Since when was Bootsy interested in art?'

'We didn't bother with the pictures, mister,' she explained patiently. 'We saw the stuffed animals an' things like that. Then the rain stopped, so we left an' had a walk in the park.'

But the Galleries were back in it again.

'While you were there, Rose, what happened? Try and remember – all of it.'

'Well –' she managed a wry smile – 'we had a laugh about one of those Egyptian mummies they've got. Bootsy said it looked the way my dad does once he has had a few beers.'

Thane kept down a grin. 'What else, Rose? How about people – was anyone there he knew?'

For a moment she sat silent and puzzled. Then, suddenly, she gave a quick, emphatic nod. 'Yes, Bootsy saw someone. That's right – I remember, because I thought maybe it was the girl. But it was the man with her that Bootsy recognized. He was a big man, grey-haired, a lot older than the girl. And I think she had sort of coppery hair.'

126

'Did you speak to them?' asked Thane sharply.

'Us?' She shook her head emphatically. 'They walked right past like we didn't exist. But Bootsy said something about the man. Something about him being a gambler an' that . . .'

'That what?'

'I'm trying to remember.' The girl bit her lip, frowning. 'It was something about the man having a business deal lined up with Mr Durman. I – well, I didn't pay much attention, mister. I was more interested in seeing if it had stopped raining.'

'But you'd know the man and girl again?'

'I think so.' She sighed and nodded. 'Why? Does it matter?'

'It might,' he said vaguely, getting to his feet. But if the couple were Jarrold Walsh and his daughter it might matter a lot. 'I'll let you know, Rose.'

She saw him to the door. The duty car was parked outside the tenement and as he climbed back aboard, Erickson glanced round at him from behind the wheel.

'Where now, sir?'

'Kelvingrove Art Galleries.' He saw Erickson's eyebrows twitch, and added stonily: 'I feel like some culture.'

'Yes, sir.' Erickson carefully blanked his face. He'd long ago learned that it usually paid.

Years had passed since Colin Thane had last gone inside the Kelvingrove Galleries but the place didn't seem to have particularly changed in the interval.

He walked into the vast main hall, where heavy, gilded chandeliers hung from the high, vaulted blue and gold ceiling and stopped beside a notice-board which informed him that the Subject of the Month was pottery. The area immediately in front of him

127

held an exhibition of religious wood-carvings and the only sound was the crisp note of footsteps as a uniformed attendant went past.

There were other people about. Two girls who looked like students were sketching beside one of the larger wood-carvings and a handful of other visitors were wandering around.

But the ground floor was mostly museum territory, and the art collections were displayed in the long galleries above. Tracy Walsh had said the Dutch paintings – with luck, he might find her there.

A broad stone stairway led to the upper level, where the introductory offering was a striking, purple-draped presentation of Kelvingrove's cherished Dali flanked by a couple of Rodin bronzes. Another time and he might have stopped, but he ignored them and walked on until he spotted the Dutch room.

Reaching it, Thane stopped in the doorway. It was a long, narrow room, the walls heavy with paintings, and a few carved wooden benches were arranged in a line down the middle of the floor.

Tracy Walsh was there as he'd hoped – but so was Roy Davidson. The only people in the room, they were sitting side by side on one of the benches and deeply engaged in an earnest, low-voiced discussion.

'Is it a private meeting, or can I join in?' he asked more cheerfully than he felt.

Startled, they broke off and swung round. The girl flushed and Davidson managed to grin weakly.

'You get around, Chief Inspector,' said Davidson with an effort. 'This wouldn't have been my idea of your scene.'

'It might be, if I had time,' shrugged Thane. 'Right now I'm working.'

'That means you're looking for me, I suppose?' asked Tracy Walsh, her grey eyes troubled.

Thane nodded.

'Why?' demanded Davidson. He glanced at the girl then rose determinedly to his feet. 'Look, Tracy hasn't done anything.'

'Then she hasn't anything to worry about.' Thane saw an easel with a canvas propped beyond the bench and nodded towards it. 'Yours, Tracy?'

'Yes.'

'Let's have a look.' He strolled over. The canvas, half-completed, was an attempt in oils to capture a general view of the room and seemed a difficult exercise in perspectives. 'Whose idea was this one?'

'Not mine.' She brushed a strand of loose hair from her forehead and left a smudge of orange paint from her fingers in the process. 'I drew it as a class assignment.'

'But you're in good company.' He gestured towards the nearest of the paintings. It was Rembrandt's masterpiece 'Man in Armour', railed off from the rest as a mild security measure and long established as one of the Galleries' proudest possessions. 'They don't come better.'

'Chocolate-box stuff,' she muttered, unimpressed.

He grinned. 'I'm no critic. How long have you been working on your own epic?'

'A couple of weeks, between lectures – and I'll be glad when I'm finished. People look in on me like I was an animal in a zoo.' She gestured towards Davidson. 'That's why Roy comes along, to cheer me up.'

'That's right,' agreed Davidson quickly and gave a nervous tug at his wisping beard. 'But I've got lectures of my own. I – maybe I should be getting back now.'

'Take a moment.' Thane turned his back on the Rembrandt. 'Any other friends been visiting you, Tracy?'

'Here?' She looked blank. 'No.'

'How about your father?'

'Yes, he came a couple of times. But he couldn't get away fast enough.' She smiled wryly. 'His idea of art is a good poker-player.'

'There's art in everything.' Thane stuck his hands in his pockets and came nearer. 'Your father seems pretty proud of you.'

'I – yes, I suppose he is.' She moistened her lips. 'Are you working round to saying something, Chief Inspector?'

'Maybe.' He stayed silent for a moment. 'That man you saw killed on the road outside here yesterday – did you know him, Tracy?'

'No.' Her eyes widened apprehensively. 'Should I have?'

'He worked for Harry Durman,' said Thane softly. He turned to Davidson. 'So we're working on two murders now – plus an attempted murder if you're willing to count a cop who was nearly killed last night.'

Davidson swallowed but stayed silent.

'Trouble has a habit of snowballing.' Thane considered them impassively. 'Sometimes it makes sense to get rid of it while you can. I think both of you know what I mean – and believe me, trying to hold back is only going to make things worse.'

It was the girl who spoke first, her voice suddenly flat and tired.

'Tell him, Roy. Let's get it over with – he's right.'

Face pale, Davidson didn't answer for a moment. Then he gave a slow, almost miserable shrug.

'If that's what you want, Tracy.'

'Well?' asked Thane.

'I've been holding back on something.' The young, bearded face opposite him twisted ruefully. 'All right, I'll do it your way. But it means I'll be kicked out of my degree course.'

130

'Worse things can happen.' It was Thane's turn to be puzzled. 'Go on.'

'Harry Durman had a problem and asked me to find the answer.' Davidson shifted his feet awkwardly. 'I did – but not on my own. I took it along to one of my professors at university and he – well, he turned it into a class project!'

Thane blinked. 'What kind of problem?'

'How to make really good chemical smoke pellets, small ones. Harry said he needed them as a gimmick in a model engineering display.'

'Did you believe him?'

Davidson shrugged. 'I believed the fifty quid he offered me. I'm on a student grant and even with a part-time job money doesn't stretch far. Not when . . .' He stopped awkwardly.

'Not when you've a girl like Tracy to take around?' suggested Thane bluntly.

'He didn't need to do it, not for me!' protested Tracy Walsh angrily. 'If I'd known, it wouldn't have happened.'

'But it did.' Davidson suddenly looked very young and crestfallen. 'I'm sorry I did it – you know that, Tracy. But those pellets are still for real.' He glanced at Thane again. 'I ran off a whole batch for him.'

'How many?'

'About thirty, and he paid up,' Davidson said uneasily. 'After he was killed, when Carl Jordan told us how he'd bought him electronic gear – well, that's when I began to sweat.'

'What size are the pellets?' asked Thane resignedly.

'About the same as a cigarette filter tip. I ended up with half a dozen senior staff helping out, all thinking it a real fun thing.' Davidson bit his lip. 'We tried them out. One pellet will blanket a fair-sized room.'

'A real fun thing,' agreed Thane dryly. 'All right, who else knows they were for Durman?'

'Just Carl – and we only told him yesterday,' said Tracy Walsh. 'Chief Inspector, couldn't it stay that way?'

'I doubt it.' Thane eyed her pensively. 'What about your father, Tracy – does he know?'

She shook her head. 'I wouldn't dare risk it. He'd go through the roof.'

He turned back to Davidson. 'And you're positive you've no idea what Durman was doing?'

'No. If I had, I'd tell you.' Davidson puffed his cheeks mournfully. 'Right now, all I want is a way out of this mess.'

'There will be,' declared Tracy Walsh with a stubborn confidence. 'You'll see.'

Thane looked at them again and sighed. 'All right, the one thing you'll both do is keep quiet about this. And I'll talk to you again. Understood?'

They nodded earnestly.

Turning on his heel, he left them and could almost feel their relief as he went out into the corridor. Smoke pellets – he knew one more item of the armoury of equipment which had been gathered. And still wasn't any nearer guessing where they'd be used.

A little way along, a bulky, middle-aged man in a grey business suit was peering at a showcase of pottery figures. But as Thane reached him the man abandoned the pretence and stepped firmly into his path.

'Chief Inspector . . .'

Thane stopped and saw two uniformed attendants hovering a few yards away.

'I'm John Randolph, security officer for the Galleries.' The man nodded past him. 'Everything all right back there?'

'In the Dutch room?' Thane blinked. 'I've no problems.'

'Good.' The security man relaxed a little. 'I wondered. Ah – these two youngsters seem all right and we've seen the girl often enough. But the camera picture had us worried.'

'The camera picture?' Thane raised an eyebrow then understood. 'I hadn't heard. How long since you started closed circuit monitoring?'

'A little while.' Randolph looked faintly embarrassed. 'The TV cameras we use are fairly well hidden. In fact, we'd have been annoyed if you'd spotted the one in there. But the man on duty at our monitoring control is an ex-policeman and recognized you. Then – well, he thought I'd better know. We've already had a general warning from our Divisional C.I.D. people to be on our toes.'

'You can get down off them for now,' said Thane dryly.

'That's a relief.' Turning, Randolph signalled the attendants. As they went away, he added quickly. 'Don't worry about anything that was said, Chief Inspector. The room isn't wired for sound – that would be an invasion of privacy. There's – ah – just the cameras and a few other things in case people are naughty.'

'So you feel your security is fairly good?' queried Thane.

'It has to be, night and day.' Randolph smiled proudly. 'We've plenty to guard.'

'I'd noticed.' Thane considered him thoughtfully. 'Randolph, you could do me a favour. Get your monitoring desk to keep a particular eye on the Dutch room from now on.'

Randolph's eyes widened. 'I thought you said . . .'

'Just an eye,' soothed Thane. 'I only want to know if other people come visiting the girl. Could you fix it?'

'I suppose so.' Randolph relaxed again. 'At least,

we can try – we're more concerned with exhibits than people and the cameras are on fixed focus. As long as you remember that if there's any kind of security problem here I've got to be told.'

'You will be, believe me,' said Thane reassuringly. 'Stop worrying – and call me if the girl has visitors.'

He left Randolph and made his way towards the exit.

Buddha Ilford had called a special Headquarters conference at noon for all Divisional C.I.D. chief inspectors. It lasted a full couple of hours, split equally between the problems raised by the Scotland and Holland game and the special watch procedures operating again for Operation Mink.

He ended with a rumbling general warning to them all.

'Just remember the uniformed branch are going to have their hands full dealing with football fans and C.I.D. still have to give them the usual back-up in case of trouble. That means man-power will be strained to the limit – every available officer will be needed, either at Hampden or on the security watches.'

A Southern Division man raised a wary hand and caught Ilford's attention. Hampden Park was in Southern Division territory and even with the reinforcements being drafted they'd have a frantic night ahead.

'Sir, if it comes to a crunch we'll have a problem in priorities.'

'Then you'll be like me for once and play it by ear,' snarled Ilford. 'Next question.'

There was an absolute silence, during which an orderly quietly entered and placed a message slip in front of Ilford. The C.I.D. chief glanced at it then turned again to his audience.

'That's all,' he said heavily, then signalled Thane to stay as the others began straggling towards the door.

'Sir?' Thane faced him.

'The latest report on Jarrold Walsh.' Ilford looked at the message slip in his hand again, crumpled it, and threw it away. 'Right now he's shopping in Sauchiehall Street with the Blantyre woman – and they've bought a dish-washer. How does that match your ideas?'

Thane shrugged. 'I still think we've got to watch him, sir.'

'Because you can't come up with anything better?' Ilford shook his head and sighed. 'Man, this morning I had Records double-check their files on the whole Walsh family and their assorted friends. We've nothing on any of them – they're honest citizens, one and all.'

'Or they've never been caught,' murmured Thane.

'It amounts to the same thing,' snapped Ilford. 'For your additional information, Walsh's son is at work at the Silk Slipper Club, the Blantyre woman's brother is drinking with some theatricals at a bar in town and – well, you know where the Walsh girl is.'

Thane raised a surprised eyebrow. 'I thought you said we couldn't cover them all, sir?'

'I did. And we can't – but I decided we'd try a sampling before this damned football madness gets under way. Not that it did any good.' Ilford glanced at his watch. 'And now I've got to go and explain to the Chief Constable exactly how we're going to try and cope with tonight. Eaten yet?'

Thane shook his head.

'Then you can buy me a beer,' said Ilford heavily. 'And we're not going to mention football, cops, or neds. Right now, I've had my fill of all three. Just hope we win, Thane. Then the fans will treat the Dutch like long-lost brothers. But if we lose you'll see sporting Scotland at its finest – God help us.'

They had beer and sandwiches at a little hole-in-the-wall bar a few minutes' walk from Headquarters and even there several tartan-tammied football fans were in evidence. Ilford stayed about fifteen minutes, then, finishing his beer and wiping a hand across his lips, he set off gloomily for his new meeting.

Left on his own, Thane lit a cigarette and drew on it pensively.

Ilford was right, as usual. They were already doing all they could but still getting nowhere. Unless a real break came their way, the next move would have to come from Ziggy Fraser and whoever was pulling the strings behind him.

And then, Ilford-style again, they'd have to play it by ear.

Jarrold Walsh came tendrilling back into his mind. He sighed and flicked ash from the cigarette, still unable to remember where he'd come across the gambling club owner before. Somehow, deep down, he knew it mattered. But just why wouldn't surface.

'Then damned well go and ask him . . .'

He said it aloud and angrily, saw the nearer football fans and the barman eye him oddly, and gave a sheepish grin. Anyway, Walsh was still on his shopping tour.

But his son would be at the Silk Slipper Club. That might be worth a try, even if only to sample Frank Walsh on his own.

It was a warm, sunny afternoon outside and the streets were beginning to fill with aimless, wandering groups of football supporters wearing team favours and idling away the time until evening came round. They marched along singing, blowing bugles, bursting into cheers whenever they saw a pretty girl and exchanged good-natured insults with anyone willing.

Taking a taxi across town, Thane watched and wondered how it would be after the game, how many of them would end up in hospital or a police cell for the night – and how many empty seats would be left aboard the charter planes when they began taking off again in the morning.

At least that part wasn't his worry.

He paid off the taxi at the club and went in. This time there was no fuss from the doorman, but as the elevator door closed he glimpsed the man already using the internal telephone.

On the top floor, he stepped out to find the gaming area unlit and deserted. But a light was burning over at the office suite and he headed there then knocked on the door.

'It isn't locked,' came Frank Walsh's muffled voice from the other side. 'Come on in, Chief Inspector.'

He did. The club owner's son was at a desk in the outer office, all alone, with several account books spread around him and a small adding machine at his right hand.

'Give me a moment. I'm just finishing trying to figure out last night's take.' Walsh tapped a few keys on the adding machine then sat back and considered the result. 'That's not going to make the old man happy, believe me!'

'Somebody on a winning streak?' queried Thane.

'Would you believe a couple of Dutch football fans?' Walsh grimaced at the memory. 'We had a bunch of them in last night – these two practically cleaned us out.'

He flicked the account books shut, then faced Thane. 'Well, still prowling?'

'Something like that.' Thane sat in one of the leather

armchairs opposite the desk. 'But – well, this is more curiosity. Your father said he met me a few years back . . .'

'But you still can't remember and he hasn't told you?' Walsh gave a sardonic grin. 'That's one of his favourite little tricks. Want me to help?'

'Yes.'

'It was ten years ago. According to the old man, he was spectating at a big poker game in a private club when it was raided and – ah – there was a bit of a general rumpus.' Walsh chuckled his amusement. 'Then there was what he calls a misunderstanding about whether he'd thumped a cop who was with you. But someone else straightened it out and once he'd cooled down he decided not to sue.'

It came back, clicking suddenly into place. He'd been a newly promoted detective sergeant, drafted in to beef up the raiding party – and he'd been saved from real trouble by an elderly inspector, long since retired.

But he could also remember the reason for the raid. There had been a tip a man they wanted might be there. A man who had been only a name to Thane at the time and who, inevitably, had got away through a back window.

An up-and-coming ned named Ziggy Fraser.

'Satisfied?' asked Frank Walsh, still grinning.

'At least I know.' Thane gave a rueful shrug, then nodded towards the account books. 'How much more of this will you get once your father re-marries?'

'Meaning will he slide out gracefully?' Walsh shook his head. 'He's not the type – anyway, as far as he's concerned I'm still wet behind the ears.'

Thane made a sympathetic noise. 'I wondered. At his age some people might have packed it in and gone off to live abroad.'

'Not a chance,' said Frank Walsh grimly. 'Anyway, Ruth isn't the type who'd want that.'

'How do you feel about him marrying her?' asked Thane mildly.

Walsh stroked a pensive finger along the desk. 'As I see it, that's none of my business. I get along with her, so does Tracy – and even "uncle" Don could be useful here.' He pursed his lips. 'We've each our own life to lead.'

'True.' Thane got to his feet. 'Has your father got round to learning that yet?'

'Ask me another time,' said Walsh shortly. 'But not now. I'm going to tonight's game with him, and I've got a load of work to finish before I can get out of here.'

Millside was far enough away from the Hampden football routes to be almost unaffected and Thane got back to the police station by late afternoon to find the atmosphere strangely peaceful. Uniform Branch were already down to skeleton strength, their spare man-power transferred to help Southern Division on crowd control, and a few of his C.I.D. team were also missing from their desks.

Phil Moss was on the telephone when he entered his office. Winking at him, Moss spent a moment longer on the line, then hung up with a sigh of relief.

'Another for the list.' Moss pencilled a name at the bottom of a long column already noted on the sheet in front of him. '"Best wishes to Sergeant Lang" – what I'd like to know is how Francey ever had time to meet them all.'

'That's community involvement.' Thane glanced down the sheet and gave a mild whistle of surprise at some of the names. 'Yes, he gets around.'

'Any more of them and I indent for an answering service,' complained Moss, dropping into a chair by the window and scratching his scrawny chest. 'You should take another look at his room in hospital. The place is like a damned flower show now – the pollen count must be at danger level.'

Thane grinned. 'How is he, Phil?'

'Sleeping off his second visit to the operating theatre. The surgeon who did the job seems happy enough.'

'Good.' Thane checked the separate list of telephone messages waiting by his desk-pad. One was from the Art Galleries. Tracy Walsh had left at three p.m. and no one else had made contact with her in the Dutch room. None of the other messages seemed to shriek for attention.

'What's the sudden interest in the Walsh girl?' queried Moss.

'Something that turned up.' Thane perched on the edge of his desk. 'I'll tell it from the beginning – it's easier that way.'

Moss listened in silence, apart from a grunt at the mention of smoke pellets and a surprised sniff as Thane finished with his memory of the long-ago poker game raid.

'Don't rely too much on that,' he warned acidly. 'It doesn't mean Jarrold Walsh ever met Ziggy Fraser.'

'I know. But – well, it's an odd coincidence.' Thane left it at that. 'And you?'

'Bits and pieces, nothing earth-shattering.' Moss scratched his chest again, then sighed. 'Either they've got fleas in that file-room or it's time my damned landlady changed the sheets again. Anyway, I dug through the arson squad's file, like you asked, then poked around a few places. There was one line on the Sapphire bingo hall fire that never did get anywhere

– a report of a car seen stopped near it for a couple of minutes around midnight.'

'Before the fire?'

'Just before. Two witnesses remembered the car and thought there was a man fiddling with something behind the wheel, but it was all vague stuff.'

'Or it was then.' Thane thought of Harry Durman and his remote control gadgets. 'What else?'

Moss shrugged. 'Well, there had been a genuine offer for the bingo hall, like Durman claimed. A development company wanted it – and as the insurance company paid out in full and own the site they're trying to make a direct deal there. They say they can get planning permission to build an office block.'

'That'll give them a sweet profit.' Thane had heard the kind of rents being charged for new office accommodation around Glasgow. Some made highway robbery modest by comparison. 'Anything on Durman?'

'Some motor-trade gossip that's drifting around. It says Durman Motors was nearly bankrupt before the fire and he was in trouble all round. The guess is he fended off the really impatient creditors by milking money from the bingo hall.'

'Then told Jarrold Walsh the bingo hall was losing money?' Thane grimaced. 'If Walsh ever guessed that was going on . . .'

'He'd have cut his throat,' agreed Moss cheerfully. 'That's my lot. For now, anyway. My feet got sore.'

'I'll get you a medal,' said Thane dryly. But he knew the few facts represented a long, slogging day's work, the kind usually forgotten by people outside. 'It all helps, Phil.'

He ran his finger down the list of telephone messages again, just to make sure. One call, marked 'Not urgent' had been from Dan Laurence at the Scientific

Bureau. Thane stopped at it, then curiosity won and he reached for the telephone.

It took a couple of minutes to get through to the Bureau chief and Laurence sounded unusually apologetic when he finally came on the Headquarters end of the line.

'It was more a blether I wanted than anything,' confessed Laurence. 'We've finished at the scrapyard in Fidra Street, but there's not much from there you don't know already. Eh – on the other hand, remember that mink coat business?'

'You think I'm likely to forget?' Thane winced and glanced at Phil Moss. 'We're forming a rabbit-hating club over here.'

'Mink, rabbit, it's all the same,' said Laurence gloomily. 'One of my electronics contacts looked in again and I started telling him about Phil's fur-sampling. Except he didn't think it was funny – he asked me if I never read anything outside of the sports pages.'

'Get to it, Dan,' pleaded Thane wearily.

'You won't believe it,' said Laurence sadly. 'Wear a thick fur coat and you'll beat almost any vibration sensor system.'

'Say that again?' Thane stared at the mouthpiece.

'It's true. I found an Interpol circular about it.' Laurence's voice became almost miserable. 'A gang in France did a couple of major jewellery raids that way, and started things. The fur damps down any air movement enough to let a man reach the sensor unit and put it out of action. Sorry, Colin – I know it sounds crazy, but it happens to be fact.'

'Here endeth today's little lesson,' said Thane wearily. He thanked Laurence, put the receiver down and turned to Moss. 'Dan thinks we're looking for a ned in a mink coat.'

'For real?' asked Moss incredulously.

'That's what he reckons.' Thane felt a growing conviction that the world was going mad. 'So all we've got to do is find one.'

Suddenly, Moss swore and sat bolt upright. 'Jarrold Walsh, damn him. His first wife – she might have had one, and if he just kept it after she died . . .'

Thane eyed him bleakly. 'How do we find out without a search warrant? And who in his right mind is going to give us one on what we've got?'

Moss sighed and subsided.

'Nothing else?' he asked.

Thane shook his head.

'Then I know what I'm going to do,' muttered Moss, scowling. 'The Hampden game is being covered live on TV – and the communications mob have a colour set rigged downstairs. They could squeeze us in.'

It seemed a good idea.

Neither of them could be expected to guess that the raid tagged 'Operation Mink' was already under way.

Chapter Seven

The Scotland v. Holland kick-off was scheduled for eight p.m. and as early as five o'clock the rush was on towards Hampden Stadium. By coach and special trains, taxis and private cars, football fans began pouring out in their thousands.

In the city their departure drained the streets of life and left only the usual big-game quota of drunks to be collected by the patrol wagons, supporters who'd celebrated too early and too well. Home fans or visitors, some determinedly clutching their team colours all the way to the cells, their night was over before it had begun.

The exodus went on while the evening stayed warm and sunny. By seven o'clock, as the real build-up reached its peak on the roads around Hampden, the prematch forecast of a one hundred thousand attendance was an established certainty.

At Millside Division even the telephones had stopped ringing and looked like staying that way until the game was over and the fans returned home. The communications room team had their TV set warmed and were building their own pre-match atmosphere by tapping the radio frequency being operated by the police mobile control at the stadium.

But other messages still came through from Headquarters Control. One arrived on Thane's desk at seven-ten p.m. Jarrold Walsh had left home and was heading in the direction of Hampden by car with two passengers aboard. A second message, suitably apologetic, came ten minutes later. The police car on shadowing duty had lost contact with Walsh's car and was bogged down in a traffic jam half a mile from the stadium.

'What did I tell you?' reminded Phil Moss with an acid triumph, between stuffing the last of a ham sandwich into his mouth. 'Be sensible, Colin – even neds take a night off. And what's good enough for them is good enough for us!'

With five minutes left before kick-off they went down to the communications room, already crammed with eager bodies. It took some vigorous elbowing to win through to a view of the screen, positioned on a platform of borrowed milk-crates.

'Any bets?' invited a loud-voiced beat sergeant who shouldn't have been there. 'I've got five quid that says Holland . . .'

He was met by a wave of indignant takers. But there was a hush as the screen showed the teams take the field, Scotland in blue jerseys and the Dutch in vivid tangerine. Someone turned up the sound, someone else switched off the overhead lights, and the roar from the packed Hampden terracing filled the room.

From the kick-off it looked as though the beat sergeant was going to collect his money, wave after attacking wave of play pounding the Scottish defence. After ten minutes of alternating groans and gasps in the room a poor clearance by Scotland's goalkeeper landed at the feet of a Dutch forward.

The ball slammed into the back of the net and the Dutch end of the terracing erupted into horn-blowing, flag-waving confusion.

The score was still that way at half-time, when the

communications room lights came on and its audience fled to check that their departments were still functioning. But they crammed back again as the interval ended, new faces here and there showing some sections were working a shift system.

Dusk outside had brought the Hampden floodlights to life. Under their glare the Dutch team resumed their attack, slashing down each wing in turn. But one careless pass, lobbed towards the centre, landed where a blue jersey was waiting. Moments later a baying roar rose from the Scottish terracing as the ball was streaked up field for a corner.

Absolute silence reigned in the communications room as Scotland's outside right took the kick, a shot which curved over the pack of players in the goalmouth and brushed past the Dutch keeper.

One all – there was back-slapping triumph among the Millside men while the cameras showed hysterical chaos in the stadium and waves of flag-waving Scotland supporters poured out on the pitch.

'Sheer luck,' grumbled the beat sergeant, looking worried while the ground was cleared and the game restarted. 'The Dutch won't let that happen again.'

The play surged back and forward and the minutes slid past while the atmosphere in the communications room became foul with cigarette smoke and charged with tension. Then a sudden howl of mass rage came from the TV set and a camera zoomed in on a Scotland forward lying writhing on the ground inside the penalty area. A caption card flashed on, showing six minutes of play to go, and the referee stood pointing firmly to the penalty spot.

A gabble of argument began in the room, to fade as the lights snapped on and a voice shouted Thane's name. He eased round, to see the night-team's desk sergeant beckoning urgently.

'Phil . . .' Nudging Moss to follow, he forced his

way back to the doorway with a sense of foreboding. The desk sergeant backed out into the corridor and waited for him there.

'Well?' asked Thane, reaching him.

'Red priority from Headquarters, sir.' The man had a message slip in one hand. 'Operation Mink.'

Red priority was reserved for major emergencies. Grimly, Thane read the scribbled telephone message and puzzled at its cryptic instruction.

'Chief Inspector Thane to Shaw Castle, Loch Lomond. Operation Mink. Rendezvous arranged with County car *en route* to collect civilian expert, John Randolph.'

Silently, he passed the slip of paper to Moss. Behind them, as the Scottish team captain strode forward to take the penalty kick at goal, the communications room door banged firmly shut.

'I've got the duty car out front, sir,' said the desk sergeant quietly. 'That's all we've got so far.'

'There'll be more.' Thane had a vague idea of Shaw Castle's location. It was an old country house-cum-fortress near the shore of the loch. 'Tell Headquarters I'm on my way.'

'Who the hell is Randolph?' demanded Moss petulantly.

'Security officer for the city Art Galleries,' said Thane and shrugged. 'The one I told you about – don't ask me how he figures in this.'

A roar of triumph thundered from the communications room.

'Ours, sir?' asked the desk sergeant hopefully.

'Ours,' agreed Thane with a wisp of a grin.

But a game was never won till it was over.

Erickson was their driver and a small transistor set propped on the dashboard kept the game with them

147

as the Jaguar sped through the quiet streets, heading west on the main Loch Lomond route. The radio commentary babbled busily, but there was no further scoring and the final whistle, backed by a roar from the stadium, made it a two-one win for Scotland.

Apart from a string of routine messages about post-match traffic patterns, Headquarters Control stayed oddly quiet with not a mention of Operation Mink. It was still that way when, a mile or so beyond the city boundary and with night coming in fast, they spotted a Dumbarton County police car stopped ahead with its hazard flashers winking. A uniformed sergeant stood beside it, waving them down.

Erickson brought the Millside car to a smart halt alongside. Briefcase clutched in one hand, face white and strained, John Randolph emerged from the County car and almost flung himself into the rear seat beside Thane.

'Go on,' he said urgently, slamming the door shut. 'Move, man.'

The Jaguar was already drawing away. Slumping back, the galleries security man turned accusing eyes on Thane.

'You said nothing would happen,' he said in a bitter, nearly trembling voice. 'Damn you, Thane, you said . . .'

'Make sense,' snapped Thane, cutting the outburst short. 'What is it, Randolph? I don't know a damned thing yet.'

Sheer disbelief showed on their passenger's face.

'Me too,' agreed Moss. He grunted and cursed as Erickson put the Jaguar round a curve in a way which sent Randolph's briefcase tumbling and all of them grabbing for support. 'What's special about this Shaw Castle?'

'You don't even know that?' Fumbling in agitation,

Randolph recovered his case from the floor. 'My God, this whole thing is like a nightmare!'

'Then wake up and talk about it,' suggested Moss caustically. 'Fair shares all round. What's at Shaw Castle?'

'The Burrell Collection,' said their passenger dispiritedly. 'Most of it, anyway – or it was till this happened.' His bitterness came wearily. 'The Burrell – have you any idea what that means, Thane?'

Colin Thane couldn't reply, feeling as if his mind had been suddenly freeze-blasted.

If you were a Scot you didn't have to be any kind of expert to have heard about the Burrell Collection. For almost thirty years it had been hanging round Glasgow's neck, one of the most ludicrously valuable albatrosses in art-world history.

He bit his lip, remembering the bones of the story. William Burrell – Sir William when he died – had been a shipping magnate whose lifelong interest had been investing in works of art. Through two world wars and most of the first half of the twentieth century he had bought shrewdly all over the world . . . translucent Chinese porcelain, Etruscan bronze, Renaissance stained glass, Gobelin tapestries and other rare items by the hundred had poured in to join paintings by Degas and Bellini, Velasquez and a score of other Old Masters.

Battling in the international auction rooms on level terms with Pierpont Morgan and Randolph Hearst, the Scottish shipping magnate had been a famed and respected connoisseur. Then, suddenly, in his eighty-third year, he had stopped and gifted the entire treasure-house collection to his native city . . . and that city hadn't known what the hell to do with it.

Half a million pounds cash came with the Burrell gift, to help build the vast gallery needed for its display. But there was one shattering proviso – the gallery must be located where its treasures were safe from smoke-polluted city air. Something easier said than done. Scheme after scheme had been proposed and abandoned over the next quarter-century while art lovers howled fury at the collection vanishing into ignominious storage and politicians learned to cringe at the name 'Burrell'.

Tyres screaming, the Jaguar took another corner hard, rasping past two shadowy, slow-moving tanker trucks. Behind the wheel, Erickson was humming to himself in the happy isolation of his own little world of speed and skill.

'Thane . . .' Randolph grew impatient.

'All right,' said Thane quietly. 'How much did they get?'

Randolph shook his head. 'Right now I can't even tell you what was out there.' He bit his lip defensively, saw Moss's expression and reacted. 'Don't think you're so clever, damn you. Can you guess how much the collection is worth?'

'No. I only collect trading stamps.' Moss shrugged unrepentant ignorance.

'A minimum, an absolute minimum, of thirty million pounds,' said Randolph sickly. 'Thirty million pounds – and it could be more. How do you price something that starts off with a job lot of twenty-two Degas originals?'

They were crushed to silence. Even Erickson forgot himself enough to come within an ace of colliding with the red lights of a tour coach. Fingers drumming on the briefcase, bitterness boiling, Randolph wasn't finished.

'If the galleries committee find the police even guessed something like this might happen then I warn you, they'll crucify every last man involved!'

'We put out a general security alert,' said Thane woodenly. 'It could have been anything from a bank job onward as far as we were concerned. And you got the warning – you told me yourself.'

'Yes.' Randolph gave a long sigh, his shoulders slumping. 'But Shaw Castle – we didn't think – it didn't seem possible!'

'That's when you've got to worry most,' muttered Moss.

The security man ignored him. 'Thane, you've got to understand the situation. There are eight thousand pieces in the Burrell Collection, eight thousand from full-sized stone archways to things the size of thimbles. We've got damned great carved doors from castles, tiny vases, tapestries rolled up like so many saleroom carpets. We've had to keep them somewhere – they've spent years crammed in attics and cellars, we've had stuff piled in old boiler-houses and corridors, anywhere we had some space.'

Thane frowned. 'But you've a gallery building now, I saw the news stories months back.'

'Right,' agreed Randolph. 'And at the same time as we started building we got Shaw Castle, a gift to the city from someone ducking death duties. It was ideal. We've been using the castle as an assembly point, bringing the collection together again there, cataloguing, cleaning, organizing it for the day the Burrell Gallery is ready.'

The last trace of dusk had vanished. Up front, Erickson had his long-range lights on and the beams carved a white tunnel down the road, a tree-lined tunnel which flickered past as the Jaguar snarled its full-power song.

Thane scowled at their radio. Headquarters Control was pumping out messages for the units covering the end of the Hampden game, with its drunks and traffic confusion and occasional brawls. But still there had been no mention of Operation Mink. Either Buddha

151

Ilford had been stunned to silence or, more likely, there still was nothing to work on.

'When did it happen – and how?' he asked.

'This evening, that's all I know.' Randolph shook his head at the memory. 'I was watching TV at home when a detective telephoned me – I can't remember his name, I didn't even believe him at first. He said the castle had been raided, a lot of stuff seemed to have been taken, and that they'd sent a car for me – I live on their side of the boundary '

'Whatever's gone, even a high-powered ned can't fence Old Masters or high-grade antiques like they were crates of whisky,' murmured Moss.

'Maybe not.' Randolph considered him grimly. 'Only an idiot steals the really major masterpieces or the carpet-sized tapestry. But there are hundreds of pieces in that collection, each of them worth a small fortune, that would be snapped up in Europe or the States – on the open market, with no way of proving they were stolen.'

'You're the expert,' said Thane wryly. He lit a cigarette and an oddly detached corner of his mind noted that for some reason his hands had a slight quiver. 'Anything else you can tell us?'

'Just that our two security men and a couple of police officers were knocked about.' Randolph peered out into the night. They had left suburbs and fields behind and were hammering along wooded, hilly countryside. 'You'll find out the rest soon enough. Another five minutes and we'll be there.'

Thane nodded. Loch Lomond lay only eighteen miles from the city. The few glimpses he'd had of Erickson's speedometer and rev counter, plus the constant booming note from the Jaguar's twin exhausts, amounted to a distance-gobbling pace.

Suddenly, the car radio came to life again.

'Operation Mink,' said the Headquarters Control

operator firmly. 'Red priority to all mobiles and stations. Look out for two large furniture vans, colour
dark blue, make and registration unknown. May be
heading towards Glasgow from the Loch Lomond
area. If seen, these should not – repeat not – be
stopped. Observe only and report. Operation Mink
message ends.'

'Ours?' asked Randolph tensely. 'I mean, those
vans . . .'

Thane nodded.

The Control operator was repeating the message
with a time of origin. A moan came from Randolph's
lips. '

'Two furniture vans – if that's how much they got
away with, I'm in trouble up to my neck.'

'Then you know the old advice,' said Moss with a
gruff attempt at sympathy. 'Stay cool and don't make
waves, Mr Randolph. Or you'll have the stuff right up
your nose.'

The turn-off from the main road towards Shaw Castle
was guarded by a County police car, its blue lamp
flashing a warning. But they'd been expected, and the
Millside car hardly had to slow as it was waved
through.

From there, half a mile of pot-holed, tree-lined
driveway ended with their first view of the castle.
Part stark medieval keep, part nineteenth-century
mansion, it was a tall silhouette against the night with
a moonlit background of the silvered waters of Loch
Lomond. Lights shone inside the building and several
police cars were drawn up around the main door.

The Jaguar drew in beside the other cars and as
they climbed out a tall man in police uniform
emerged from the castle and strode towards them.

'Which of you is Thane?' he demanded bluntly.

'I am' – Thane checked the rank badges, and saw he was a superintendent – 'sir.'

'Bert Docherty, County Constabulary.' The uniformed man grimaced at him in the moonlight. 'And forget the "sirs" tonight, Thane – we've a right going foul-up here. Did you bring the galleries security character?'

'That's him.' Thane thumbed towards Randolph, who was coming towards them. 'The other one is D.I. Moss, from my division.'

'Right.' Docherty waited bleakly for Randolph to arrive. 'Mr Randolph, the best thing you can do for now is to try to tell us what's missing. Agreed?'

Dumbly, still clutching his briefcase, Randolph nodded.

'Take him in, Phil,' said Thane. 'Stay with him.'

'Poor basket,' said Docherty wryly as Moss guided Randolph on. 'A few of us may have our heads on the chopping block over this, but he's more likely to be gutted first. Fag?'

Thane took one of the offered cigarettes. The County man struck a match, shielded the flame between his hands, and they lit up. Taking a long draw, Thane decided he'd been fortunate. There were County men and County men, some fiercely jealous of their territory. The kind with Docherty's outlook tended to be in the minority.

'We'll stay out a moment.' Docherty flicked the spent match away. 'My lads are as thick as fleas on a dog's back in there – and probably about as useful. Anyway, I could use a minute just thinking.'

He stood silent for a moment, looking out towards the loch, then gave a sigh.

'Like to hear what we've got?'

Thane nodded.

'Right. You'd hear the radio "special search"

message for those two damned vans – and that's about the only positive lead so far.'

'Can't the security guards help?' asked Thane. 'Randolph said . . .'

'Whatever he said, what happened was a damned sight different,' snarled Docherty. 'There were two night-security staff in the castle and we'd drafted in two of our own men because of the general panic – though I'm damned if anyone really thought this place would be raided. Now one of my lads is on his way to hospital with a fractured skull and the rest aren't much better.' He turned and scowled at Shaw Castle's black shape. 'As safe as a fort, we were told – well, this mob went through electronic locks, the lot, like they were carving butter.'

Grim-faced, Docherty capsuled his way through the rest of it.

Minutes after eight-thirty p.m., as the light faded, the castle's automatic fire alarm had begun ringing. Thick smoke suddenly billowed along the ground floor corridors and the guards simultaneously discovered the telephone lines were dead. While they were still trying to find out what was happening a squad of stocking-masked raiders had burst in and they'd been clubbed down.

Battered and bleeding, tied, blindfolded then dumped helplessly in a side room, the guards had heard two heavy vehicles drive up and the sounds of loading.

'Loading took half an hour, as near as they can reckon it,' said Docherty grimly. He stopped a moment, lips pursed, as a large owl flapped its way over their heads in the moonlight and landed noisily in a tree. 'The vans drove off, one of the guards managed to get loose after a spell, and – well, he hiked to the nearest farm to raise the alarm. The farm's where we had our only bit of luck. The farmer

155

told us about a cottage a couple of miles from here. It's been lying empty for months, but a couple of furniture vans arrived there this afternoon. We've checked – the vans are gone and the cottage is still empty.'

'Cool,' murmured Thane with reluctant admiration. 'Keep things looking ordinary enough and you'll get away with anything.'

'That's only half of it,' said Docherty grimly. 'They made damned sure they weren't interrupted by anyone. Another of the locals says the castle driveway was closed just before dusk – he saw two men in police uniform manning a barrier pole. Come on, I'll show you the rest.'

Thane followed the County superintendent over to the castle. Inside the main door the place seemed alive with uniformed and plain-clothes men, but Docherty bored a way through them, then halted, gesturing around. They were at the entrance to what had once been the castle's stone-flagged banqueting hall, still complete down to a dilapidated minstrels' gallery and a few ragged banners, but now lit by neon-tube lights suspended from the roof. The lights shone on rows of long trestle tables laden with packing cases, paintings, carefully rolled tapestries and a vast miscellany of dust-sheeted items.

'This is what they left,' said Docherty briefly. 'They only went for unopened crates which were mostly out in the corridors. Smell the smoke?'

Thane nodded, his nostrils catching the acrid scent hanging in the air.

'Over here,' invited Docherty. He shepherded Thane across the stone floor towards an old-fashioned metal radiator and thumbed at a small, blackened plastic tube which had been placed on a sheet of white paper beside it. 'We found that behind the radiator – and we're still looking for the others.'

Thane stooped and peered, keeping his hands in his pockets and knowing the County man was watching. One end of the tiny tube held a few burned-out fragments of chemical, the other was a tiny, transistorized receiver unit. Roy Davidson's smoke pellets combined with Harry Durman's remote control system – he sighed and glanced up.

'How did they get in?'

Docherty shrugged. 'I can make a guess. Somebody wanders up with a bag of tools, says he's been sent to do a job, and nobody bothers to check back with where he says he came from. When I find out for sure . . .' He left the threat hanging.

'And the alarm system?'

'Overridden all the way.' The County man paused, his mouth tightening. 'Ask the expert, not me.'

Randolph was coming towards them, Phil Moss trotting gloomily at his heels.

'Well?' asked Thane as they arrived. 'How does it look?'

'Bad, very bad.' Randolph bit his lip and looked down at something he was clutching in his right hand. 'It's difficult to be exact, Chief Inspector. All I've got is a master-list of numbered packing cases, but . . .'

'He thinks about two million quid's worth,' said Moss bluntly.

Thane heard Docherty give a noise like a groan and felt a stomach-tightening sense of having failed.

'That's only approximate,' said Randolph weakly. 'I – well, it will take time to be positive. They simply loaded the crates nearest the door and ignored anything that was bulky.'

'A sort of rag-bag grab,' suggested Moss, trying to be helpful. 'Looks like they dropped some of the stuff on the way.'

'Yes.' A sick note of anger entered Randolph's

157

voice. Slowly, he opened his hand and showed them a fragment of broken porcelain. 'This was early Ming, an octagonal vase. I saw one auctioned at Sotheby's in London last year – it fetched almost thirty thousand pounds.' He ran his other hand across his forehead, in a gesture of despair. 'Don't make it worse by suggesting we buy a tube of glue.'

'Let's talk about it, Randolph.' Thane drew him out of the path of a hurrying constable. 'How many people knew you were using Shaw Castle for gathering the collection?'

Randolph shrugged. 'A number of the galleries department staff, a few outside tradesmen and – well, one or two experts in the art world, people we asked to help us in cataloguing.'

'These experts,' said Thane thoughtfully. 'Would any of them be likely to go back afterwards and give a lecture to art students on what they'd seen?'

'They – they might. But we wouldn't have encouraged it.'

'But they might, and they'd know the security layout, maybe even mention it to keep their audience interested?' Thane saw a protest forming on the man's lips and raised a hand. 'Can't you hear it happen, Randolph? A lecturer letting his students into some "little secrets" – and maybe mentioning security gadgets like the vibration sensor equipment that was here?'

'Perhaps. Except –' Randolph looked puzzled – 'not the sensors, Chief Inspector. We installed the rest of the electronic system, but the sensors were cancelled a couple of months back. The manufacturers had taken too long to deliver.'

'Maybe even that helps,' said Thane grimly. 'Somebody didn't know they'd been cancelled. Phil, get some names from him.'

Nodding, Moss led the bewildered man away

towards a couple of chairs. As they left, Superintendent Docherty broke his long and patient silence.

'You looked like that meant something,' he said hopefully. 'If it did, you're ahead of me.'

'Call it a hunch, but one I don't like.' Thane rubbed a hand along his chin, gave a lop-sided grin, and thought of two furniture vans rumbling along with two million pounds of *objets d'art* bouncing around inside them. 'When do you reckon the vans left here?'

'At least an hour ago.' Docherty scowled at an elaborate piece of silver plate lying on one of the tables. Someone had been using it as an ashtray. 'If they were heading back into Glasgow they'd get there at about nightfall – just as the football crowds were swarming out from Hampden.'

'Have you a phone working from here?'

'We've rigged a line.' Docherty puffed his cheeks, frowning. 'Look, Thane, I've played straight with you, made it easy as I could. But this is still a County patch and . . .'

'And it stays that way,' Thane stopped him. 'I'm only thinking of the city end.'

'Fair enough.' Docherty became friendlier again. 'Anything else you want?'

Thane nodded. 'A chance to look over the cottage.'

'Help yourself. Inside, it looks like people have been using it as a base for weeks.' Docherty gestured apologetically. 'An estate agency handled the renting, but we're still trying to contact them.'

'I'll take a guess at their name,' said Thane softly. 'Horizon Real Estate?'

Eyes widening, the County man nodded.

'We know someone who works for them.' Thane left it at that, but promoted Carl Jordan close to the top of his list. 'We can handle that for you, and I'll

159

forget about going to the cottage. As soon as Moss is finished we'll head back to Glasgow.'

'You're beginning to look almost happy,' said Docherty with a touch of envy. 'What's it all about?'

'A girl and a football match,' Thane told him.

'Eh?'

'They're separate,' explained Thane. 'Separate but they add together.'

Docherty didn't argue. With two million pounds' worth of worries on his mind he hadn't time to guess riddles.

By midnight, the final count of post-Hampden arrests had reached ninety-three – most of them drunks, a few pickpockets and con men, one a befuddled optimist who had missed his last bus home and had tried to steal a police car. But the total was modest by local standards, and already the first charter flights were taking off from Glasgow Airport, ferrying Dutch fans home in less exuberant style than they'd arrived.

'That's one bolt-hole we're watching for Fraser – though the airlines are squealing about delays.' Hunched over his desk at Central Division, Chief Superintendent Buddha Ilford sucked his pipe in stolid fashion and maintained his grimly determined air of calm. 'Customs and Immigration are screwing down on every flight. Nobody is going to get as much as a half-bottle of whisky out of that place tonight and the same goes for anyone with as much as a smudge on his passport.'

Sitting opposite him, gulping scalding coffee from a mug which was inscribed Property of British Railways, Thane nodded. Every way in and out of the city was being watched. That meant the airport, rail stations, check points on the main roads – and not

160

much chance anything would come of them. But it had to be done and if the two vans used at Shaw Castle were in town neither they nor their contents were going to slip out again.

He had been back in the city for about half an hour – to find on arrival that Ilford already had at least one item tied up.

Art pundit and critic, occasional poet and dramatist, a bow-tied individual named Jeremy Garrick was currently sweating in another room in Central Division, completing a statement on how he'd lectured a class of art students after a visit to Shaw Castle – a lecture in which he now nervously admitted he'd spelled out most of the security arrangements.

With Tracy Walsh in the audience. Checking that part had involved dragging a somewhat irate studies organizer out of bed.

Thane glanced at his watch and saw Ilford raise an eyebrow.

'Moss?' asked Ilford.

He nodded. Phil Moss had dropped off at Millside Division on the way and was bringing in Carl Jordan. The estate agent's clerk had some explaining of his own to do.

Ilford drew on his pipe again till the bowl glinted cherry red. 'Well, the Walsh girl is still at home with Davidson, we've her father and the Blantyre woman tabbed at the Silk Slipper Club – and if as much as a mouse gets in or out of either place without being spotted then I'll believe in fairies.' He paused, frowning slightly. 'But that still leaves the son and brother Blantyre on the loose.'

'They could be anywhere, sir.' Victory celebrations for Scotland's win were going on all over the city. Even Buddha Ilford had a suspicion of whisky on his breath. 'Can I see that report sheet again?'

Ilford shoved it over. With Ruth Blantyre as a

161

passenger, Jarrold Walsh had driven up to the Silk Slipper Club at eleven-thirty p.m. – the first time he'd been sighted since the shadowing team had lost him in the pre-match traffic jam. Tracy Walsh and Roy Davidson had surfaced half an hour earlier, arriving at her home in Davidson's old car.

'Suppose you say it, man,' said Ilford suddenly. Taking the pipe from his mouth, he used the stem as a pointer. 'I turned down a Divisional officer's recommendation – yours. I decided not to establish a full surveillance on the Walsh tribe. If I'd done what you wanted . . .' He stopped there and shrugged.

For a moment, Thane didn't answer. Never before could he remember having seen Buddha Ilford look so old and tired. But that paunchy, heavily built figure carried a whole city on his shoulders and balanced it there in a constant gamble of personal judgement against possibility.

'It would have worked out no differently,' he said flatly. 'We'd still have had to play things by ear.'

Ilford made a quick, throat-clearing noise. 'Not that I was making any kind of apology, damn you . . .'

He broke off as the telephone rang, answered it with a grunt, then looked up.

'Moss is here. He's got Jordan with him. Want them in?'

Thane nodded and Ilford growled an affirmative into the mouthpiece then hung up.

A moment later the door opened and Moss led Carl Jordan into the room. The red-haired estate agent's clerk was pale-faced as he limped up to the desk and behind him Moss gave a slight, confirming nod.

'You know why you're here?' asked Ilford curtly.

'Yes.' Jordan bit his lip and looked down at the threadbare carpet. 'I – well, I suppose I should have told you. But I – I just didn't think it would matter.'

'Didn't you?' Ilford's attitude was acid. 'Moss?'

'Like we guessed, sir.' Moss glanced in Thane's direction. 'He did another little deal with Harry Durman on top of those electronic parts. The story was a friend of Durman's wanted to rent a cottage anywhere near the south end of Loch Lomond. So Jordan fixed him up.'

'What name went on the rent agreement?' asked Thane.

Carl Jordan turned to him like a man who'd been on the losing end of a fight for far too long.

'Somebody called John Roberts,' he said wearily. 'Harry took the rent agreement away and brought it back signed, with three months' rent in advance. I gave him the keys – that was weeks ago.'

'Did you ever see this "Mr Roberts"?'

'No.' Jordan shook his head miserably. 'Look, Chief Inspector, I kept quiet because I had my job to think about. It – well, it was legitimate business.'

'But any publicity and the boss would have thrown you out on your ear?' suggested Thane.

'He will now.' Jordan rested his hands on the desk and shook his head despairingly. 'Damn Harry Durman – everything he touched has become a foul-up.'

'Agreed,' said Ilford dryly. 'Thane?'

'Dump him outside, Phil,' said Thane, his face expressionless but with a tendril of sympathy for the man. 'Get someone to take a statement. Then go out to Walsh's home – collect his daughter and take a look through the wardrobes.'

'I'm playing find the mink?'

Ilford nodded. 'The search warrant's waiting.'

'But all you tell her is you're looking for a fur coat, Phil,' cautioned Thane. 'That, and some questions about where she went tonight.'

'Right. And I bring her here?'

Thane shook his head. 'The Silk Slipper – I'll be there with Jarrold Walsh.'

Moss grinned and thumbed Jordan towards the door.

Chapter Eight

The Silk Slipper Club was cashing in on the night's celebrations. Cars were parked nose to tail around the brightly lit entrance and a couple of taxis were unloading another batch of customers as Thane arrived.

He had the duty car drop him a stone's throw away, left Erickson on radio watch, and was walking towards the club when a figure slipped out of a darkened doorway to join him.

'No change, sir,' reported Detective Constable Beech quietly. 'Plenty of people coming and going, but Walsh and the woman are still inside.'

'Good.' Thane looked around. 'Where's his car?'

'The club has a private garage in the basement – he left it there.' Beech's young face gave him a hopeful grin. 'I parked my car across the entry, just in case.'

'Then don't blame me if you get a traffic ticket for obstruction.' Thane considered him and chuckled. 'All right, you can do the notebook end of this one.'

Beech nodded. 'Caution and charge, sir?'

'You're joking,' said Thane dryly. 'But we're going to try what Phil Moss would call a spot of leaning. So no smiles and no happy talk. Understood?'

Beech didn't exactly look as if he did. But he nodded, checked his notebook pocket and followed Thane in. Once past the doorman, they took the elevator up and shared the ride with a couple in evening dress. The door sighed open, they stepped out on the top floor, and a babble of noise met their ears.

The club was crowded, every game in full swing, and the steady thump of one-armed bandit handles along one wall was almost drowned by the steady rattle of an automatic money-changing machine operating beside the other. Round the tables, each spin of the wheel or rattle of dice brought a shout of laughter or groans of mock despair.

Usually the city took its gambling seriously. But this night, at least, the atmosphere was close enough to carnival.

They pushed their way through towards the office suite, where a flunkey in evening dress moved to bar their way but fell back as Thane showed his warrant card.

'Straight through, Chief Inspector.' The man grinned apologetically and opened the door. 'The boss has put the shutters up as far as this mob is concerned.'

Thane pulled Beech on, interrupting the latter's interested study of a blonde in an almost see-through white trouser suit who was clutching a fistful of money. As they crossed the outer office, where a couple of shirt-sleeved clerks were busy, Jarrold Walsh appeared at the inner doorway.

'Back again?' The club owner's attitude fell a few degrees short of a friendly welcome. He stuck his hands deep in the pockets of the tweed suit he was wearing and glanced at Beech. 'Started an apprentice?'

'This is Detective Constable Beech,' said Thane stonily. 'We'd like to talk.'

Walsh stood back and let them pass, closing the door once they'd entered the room. Curled up in one of the leather armchairs, Ruth Blantyre greeted them with a resigned smile. She was in a simple but expensive wool dress and had kicked off her shoes.

'Looking for a drink?' asked Walsh bluntly, gesturing towards an open cocktail cabinet.

'Jarrold.' The woman frowned a protest and uncurled, smoothing down her skirt as she rose. 'Go easy.'

'Well, damn it, how much longer till we get the police force off our backs?' demanded Walsh irately. But as their eyes met he shrugged and gave in. 'All right, Ruth – your way. Chief Inspector, can I offer you and Boy Friday a drink?'

'Not right now.' Thane said it neutrally, but Ruth Blantyre's frown switched his way.

'Any special reason why you're here?' she asked, her manner altering.

Thane nodded.

'Then it can wait till I'm ready.' Jarrold Walsh reached deep into the cocktail cabinet, produced a bottle of milk, and poured himself a glass. He turned with the glass in his hand, thawing a little. 'I was at the Scotland–Holland game tonight – shouted my head off like everyone else. Now my damned ulcer's throbbing.'

'I saw some of the game on TV,' said Thane mildly. 'It looked pretty good.'

'Half our team played like rubbish. As for our first goal, that was sheer damned luck.' The club owner took a gulp of the milk. 'Still, forget it. You didn't come here to talk football. But if it's anything more about Harry Durman, then you've already got all I know.'

'Not Durman.' Thane shook his head. 'I want to talk about your daughter.'

'Tracy?' Walsh's eyes widened behind the thick spectacles and his manner froze again. 'What about her? If anything has happened . . .'

'She's at home,' said Thane shortly. 'Or she was –
I'm having her brought over here.'

Walsh stayed very still for a moment, the glass in
his hand forgotten.

'You'd better sit down,' he said grimly. 'I want to
know what the hell is going on.'

'But – but you're sure Tracy's all right?' asked Ruth
Blantyre anxiously, moving closer to Walsh.

'As far as I know, yes.' Thane settled in one of the
chairs, Beech followed his example. 'That's not what
I meant.'

'I didn't think it was,' said Walsh harshly. 'Sit
down, Ruth.'

She obeyed, concern on her face, but the club owner
stayed on his feet and took another quick drink from
his glass.

'What about Tracy?' he demanded.

'Has she been with you tonight?' asked Thane.

'No.' Suddenly, Walsh noticed that Beech had his
notebook out and had begun writing. 'What the hell's
he doing?'

'Taking a verbatim note, unless his shorthand
breaks down.' Thane met the man's glare calmly. 'Did
she tell you where she would be this evening?'

Walsh chewed his lip and glanced towards Ruth
Blantyre.

'Some disco club in town,' she said. The woman
shrugged apologetically. 'That's all she told me,
Jarrold, except that she was going out with Roy.'

'That long-haired creep?' Walsh's nostrils flared
angrily. 'If Davidson has landed Tracy in some kind of
trouble . . .'

'Jarrold – let them tell it.' Ruth Blantyre stopped
him short. She turned to Thane, fingering her engagement ring with a hint of nervousness. 'Go on, Chief
Inspector.'

'Thank you.' Thane fixed his attention on Walsh.

'If you want it formally, your daughter and Roy Davidson jointly held back information concerning Durman's death. We now have reason to believe they may also be able to help us in inquiries into another matter.'

Sheer disbelief on his face, Walsh stared at him. 'What other matter?' he asked hoarsely.

'An armed raid on a place called Shaw Castle,' said Thane bluntly. 'Ever heard of it?' He didn't wait for an answer. 'Right now it happens to be the temporary home of part of the Burrell Collection – except now they're missing two van-loads of some of the priciest antiques in the world, from silver and gold plate through to porcelain and crystal. And four men who were guarding it are in hospital.'

Despairingly, Walsh combed a hand through his thick white hair. With his other hand, he slammed the glass of milk down on the desk.

'Ruthy, tell this man he's off his head!' he appealed.

'That's not how we see it,' said Thane. 'So do we talk sensibly?'

'Talk?' Walsh's voice became quiet but the words stabbed like so many needles. 'Thane, when Tracy gets here I'm going to have a lawyer and she says nothing without him agreeing. And afterwards – God help you for this.'

'You've a phone,' shrugged Thane. 'Call any lawyer you want. But if you do, then when Tracy gets here I march her straight back through the middle of that crowd outside, under open escort, and we talk in the police station.'

'You bastard . . .' Walsh's fists clenched in fury.

'It's your choice,' said Thane calmly.

'Jarrold –' Ruth Blantyre's face was pale, but she spoke determinedly – 'you should do it his way, for Tracy's sake.'

'All right,' surrendered Walsh bitterly, then scowled at Beech, who was still scribbling. 'But he stops first.'

'Take a rest, Beech.' Thane hid a smile at Beech's relief as he stopped, then turned back to Jarrold Walsh. 'When did you last see Tracy?'

'At home, this evening, before I went to the game,' snarled Walsh.

'And you went with him, Miss Blantyre?' asked Thane.

She shook her head. 'I was at the house, but I stayed. Frank and my brother left with Jarrold to see the match – and Tracy, I think she left about an hour later.'

'Then what did you do?'

'Watched TV for a spell, though there was only the match on every channel, then went into town to meet Jarrold for a meal, like we'd arranged. Frank and Don were there too' – she grimaced slightly – 'and Jarrold turned up eventually.'

Thane raised an eyebrow and tried to keep his apparent interest low-key as he turned to Walsh again. 'So you didn't stay together?'

'We got separated in the crowd outside the ground,' said Walsh remotely. 'You could have lost a regiment in that kind of crush.'

'At least they knew where to meet you afterwards,' murmured Thane. 'They didn't stay with you after the meal?'

'This is Frank's night off. Don took him to a party somewhere.' Walsh scowled impatiently. 'What the hell's any of this got to do with Tracy?'

'I like to place people. As far as you know, none of you has seen her since she left the house – correct?'

Tight-lipped, Walsh nodded.

'Good,' murmured Thane. Expression unchanged,

he leaned forward. 'How well does she know Ziggy Fraser?'

For a moment, Jarrold Walsh seemed incapable of speech then he gave an incredulous sound that was meant to be a laugh.

'So you remembered? And that's how you're trying to tie her in?' He swung towards Ruth Blantyre. 'Ziggy Fraser is a ned, Ruthy – a cheap four-by-two thug.'

'But you know him,' said Thane grimly.

'Like I knew Harry Durman,' snapped Walsh. 'For the same reason. We were born in the same stinking street, we went to the same lousy school – but that's as far as it goes. Tracy hasn't even heard about him.'

The room door had clicked open as he spoke. From behind them came a sudden question.

'Tracy hasn't heard about who?'

They turned. An old raincoat loose over her shoulders, her face pale but defiant, Tracy Walsh came in with Moss at her elbow.

'Who haven't I heard about?' she asked again.

Jarrold Walsh took three long, swift steps and reached her side. An arm round her shoulders, he glared at Moss.

'If you've laid any kind of hand on her, Moss, God help you,' he grated. 'Tracy, how do you feel?'

'How do you expect?' she said wearily. 'But don't come the heavy, Dad. Not right now.'

Lips pursed, he nodded. 'Come and sit down.'

She did, glancing wryly at Thane as she passed and perching on the arm of Ruth Blantyre's chair.

'Who don't I know?' she asked for a third time.

'A man named Ziggy Fraser,' said Thane. 'Ever heard of him, Tracy?'

She shook her head. 'He sounds like a footballer.'

171

'He isn't.' Thane glanced past her towards Moss. 'Phil?'

'No trouble,' reported Moss laconically. 'Except maybe having to tug her loose from Davidson. He wanted to come with us.'

Jarrold Walsh grunted. 'That's the first decent thing I've heard about him. Tracy . . .'

'Not now,' said Thane curtly, cutting him short. 'You searched the house, Phil?'

'Uh-huh.' Moss saw Walsh's expression and added blandly, 'With a warrant in one hand – and nothing got broken.' He paused ard shrugged. 'No luck.'

'Am I allowed to ask what the hell you were looking for?' demanded Jarrold Walsh bitterly.

'That part goes back to Harry Durman's murder,' said Thane. Getting to his feet, he crossed towards them. 'Did your first wife own a mink coat?'

Walsh seemed bewildered. 'Yes.'

'What happened to it?'

'Dad –' Tracy tugged at her father's arm – 'they looked in that wardrobe. But – but the coat isn't there, or anywhere else.'

For a moment Walsh said nothing, then he gestured impatiently. 'I know that. I – I sold the thing. Didn't I tell you?'

She shook her head.

'Then I meant to – you didn't want it, though I asked you often enough. Now I'm marrying Ruth there was no sense in keeping it. You don't mind, do you?'

'No.' Tracy still seemed surprised. 'I just didn't know.'

'Who bought it?' asked Moss from the background.

'None of your damned business,' snapped Walsh.

'Leave it, Phil,' murmured Thane. 'Tracy, where were you tonight?'

172

'At a disco in town with Roy – the place we always go, the Yellow Pearl. Then straight home.'

'And like last time, half the people there will confirm it?' asked Thane dryly.

She nodded.

Relieved, Jarrold Walsh gave a sigh. 'Thank God for that.' Then his mouth firmed again. 'Tracy, I've a few questions of my own to ask. Thane says you and Davidson knew something about Durman's murder and kept quiet. Is that right?'

'Yes.' She flushed. 'I – we were going to tell you.'

'I should damned well think so.' Walsh ran a slow hand across his forehead then turned to Thane again. 'Well, what more do you want?'

Thane shrugged. 'I'm finished for now.'

He signalled Beech to his feet, but Walsh wasn't finished.

'And now you just walk out? You march in here, you search my house, you drag my daughter here against her will – and we're supposed to forget it?'

'I didn't say it was over,' said Thane softly. 'Remember that part, Mr Walsh.' He glanced at Tracy. 'Your father can tell you why it happened.'

He had the door opened and was on his way out before either of them could answer.

More customers were pouring into the Silk Slipper as they left and in the street outside a singing, horn-blowing group of football fans were weaving a happy way along the opposite pavement.

Ignoring them, Thane led the way to the Millside duty car. Stopping beside it, he looked along the street.

'Beech, move your car. I want that garage entrance clear.'

173

'Yes, sir.' Beech hesitated as if he'd something else on his mind.

'Something troubling you?' asked Thane.

'Back there . . .' Beech swallowed awkwardly. 'Well, you didn't press him about the coat. Or . . .'

'Or a whole lot more,' agreed Thane cheerfully. 'That's right. And you can forget the notes you took. Now move that car, then get back here.'

Frowning, still puzzled, Beech trotted off.

'He'll learn,' said Moss dryly. 'You left Walsh worried. How long do you reckon?'

'Before he takes off?' Thane rubbed his chin hopefully. 'Twenty minutes maybe – after he's gone through the irate father act.'

'Presuming the girl's in the clear.' Moss sucked his teeth. 'Aye, I'll buy that part. I'm not so sure about the other one.'

'Ruth Blantyre?' Thane shrugged. 'We'll find out.'

'Leaving father, son and –' Moss avoided the blasphemy with an effort – 'brother Don?'

Thane nodded. He'd played it that way, he'd kept back some of the cards he could have used, and he'd already gained more than he'd expected.

'Think any of them were at that football match?' queried Moss.

'Walsh talked like he might have been. He said that was why his gut was troubling him.'

Moss nodded wisely. 'Tension, like with me. The acid builds up.'

'Maybe.'

But there could have been a more important factor behind Jarrold Walsh's acid balance – though whether or not he'd been at the Scotland–Holland game might be hard to prove. If a man knew football and saw even part of a game on TV or heard a radio commentary he could probably discuss most of the run of play with consummate ease.

What mattered now was how much he'd worried Walsh and how fast the club owner would react.

Colin Thane's twenty minutes ticked past slowly and the street scene changed little. Behind the wheel of the duty car, Erickson hummed quietly to himself and occasionally yawned. Beech had abandoned his own car and was in the front passenger seat, leaving Thane and Moss to share the rear bench.

An occasional message murmured over from Control, but never once with the prefix Operation Mink. Two million pounds' worth of antiques and two furniture vans might as well have been swallowed up into space for all that seemed to be happening.

One a.m. slipped by and Moss's stomach began rumbling from lack of food. Then, suddenly, Beech gave a grunt of interest and pointed.

Tracy Walsh had appeared at the brightly lit entrance to the Silk Slipper. She came to the kerb, and glanced around – and a moment later, headlights glaring, her father's white Jaguar roared out of its basement garage, turned facing away from her, stopped, then reversed back to halt beside her.

They had a glimpse of a figure in soft hat and raincoat leaning across to open the passenger door. She climbed aboard, the door closed, and immediately the Jaguar roared off again.

'Not too close,' said Thane sharply as Erickson started their car. 'Just don't lose him.'

'Sir.' Erickson shot him a single glance which indicated how he felt about unwanted advice, then got to work.

There was still enough traffic around to make the task fairly easy. Ahead of them, the white Jaguar seemed to be heading west across town and it was in a hurry. Twice it bored across traffic lights in mid-change and soon afterwards it had to brake sharply and swing in as it took a corner wide and came close to colliding with a scavenging truck meandering in from the opposite direction.

The same thing happened another half-mile on and this time the Jaguar avoided a trundling milk tanker by inches.

'Look at him,' said Erickson with disgust, keeping the Millside car cruising smoothly a few vehicles behind. 'He may be a big-shot in that club, but he drives like a ruddy woman!'

It took a couple of moments for the words to sink home to Thane. Then, tight-lipped, he leaned forward and stared ahead with a sudden feeling of despair. As the white Jaguar weaved sloppily from one traffic lane to the next, he made up his mind.

'Take him, Erickson,' he said greyly. 'Now.'

Erickson raised an eyebrow but nodded. Beech and Moss exchanged equally surprised glances, then grabbed for support as the Millside car snapped down to second gear and began carving forward, siren wailing.

They took Jarrold Walsh's Jaguar about a quarter of a mile on, forcing it to a halt at the kerb. Thane was out first and yanked open the driver's door.

Ruth Blantyre met his gaze sadly, removed the man's hat she was wearing, and smoothed back her blonde hair with a grimace.

'Come out of there,' said Thane wearily, then, looking past her, 'You too, Tracy.'

They obeyed reluctantly and he beckoned them round to the front of the car. Behind him, he heard Beech give a startled exclamation and Moss mutter something to the younger man.

'Where's Jarrold, Ruth?' asked Thane grimly.

'I don't know.' She refused to be panicked. 'Neither does Tracy, so it's no use asking.'

'Then exactly what the hell were you trying to do?'

She shrugged. 'I'm taking Tracy home. That's no crime, is it?'

'No,' he agreed gloomily while Moss slouched over. 'Not on its own. But whatever Jarrold told you, grandstanding for him leaves both of you in trouble.'

They looked at him in silence, Tracy shielding her eyes as a car swept past with headlamps on full beam.

Thane tried again. 'Did he tell you about the Burrell raid, Tracy?' As she nodded, he went on bluntly: 'Funny, isn't it? You knew about Shaw Castle – and a fair amount about the security set-up.'

'So did plenty of other people!' Her head came up indignantly. 'Anyway, I didn't talk about it except at – at . . .' Her voice died away and she swallowed, suddenly avoiding his gaze.

'Except at home?' asked Moss, leaning against the Jaguar's radiator, a cynical grin on his thin face. 'Tracy, we know your father's old school pal Ziggy Fraser had a contract for the job – and that Harry Durman was working on it when he got that screwdriver through his back.'

'Jarrold hasn't done anything,' protested Ruth Blantyre angrily.

'Then why this piece of play-acting?' demanded Thane stonily.

'Because –' she glanced at the girl then sighed – 'because he was worried sick about Tracy being involved. Or you thinking she was, anyway. He – well, he seemed to think there was a way he could stop that.'

'So he goes galloping off into the night?' Thane shook his head sceptically. 'It's quite a picture.'

'It's true,' said Tracy Walsh earnestly. 'That's why he said . . .' She stopped again, uncertain.

'He said what?' Thane put all the urgency he could

177

into his voice. 'Listen, Tracy, if you believe him then you've got to believe something else. That he's dealing with a bunch that even Jarrold Walsh is going to find too tough to handle. They've murdered, they've maimed, they've got away with a small fortune – do you think they're going to put out a welcome mat when he arrives?'

A car-load of teenagers came crawling towards them. As it passed, the occupants cat-called from the opened windows then the driver accelerated rapidly.

'They think we're running a speed trap.' Thane grimaced. 'Tracy, right now maybe I'm giving you a chance to save your father from another kind of trap – one that could kill him.' He paused, the silence broken only by the sound of the receding car and the crackle from the Jaguar's cooling exhaust, then added softly: 'Even if Don and Frank are there.'

The girl gave a sound like a moan and turned to Ruth Blantyre as if pleading for help. The older woman gripped her hand then, face turned to stone, stared at Thane as if mesmerized.

'You can't mean that,' she said quietly. 'Even if they were . . .'

'I don't know,' conceded Thane. 'Do you?'

'They were all at that football game . . .'

He shrugged. 'Can you prove it?'

'Jarrold can.' There, at least, she was confident and showed it. 'He met a director he knew – they had a drink in the V.I.P. room at the interval and he brought a couple of people from there back to eat with us.'

Even Phil Moss felt the impact, levering himself up from the Jaguar's radiator with a mumble of surprise.

'You're sure?' asked Thane, the night suddenly seeming colder.

She nodded and glanced at Tracy, tightening her

grip on the girl's hand. 'You really think he's in danger? Even if . . .'

'Whoever is there. From the moment he arrives,' answered Thane positively.

Tracy Walsh brought her head up slowly, her eyes mirroring a personal nightmare, her lips struggling for a moment before she could speak.

'He wanted the keys for the old bingo hall, Chief Inspector,' she said haltingly.

'Why?'

'Because he knows Frank has been there lately.'

Thane nodded, knowing what it had cost her and seeing the mixture of relief and despair on Ruth Blantyre's face.

'Beech . . .'

'Sir?' Beech came forward awkwardly.

'Stay with them and take them home. You know where we'll be.'

Beech watched him get back aboard the police car with Moss. As the car started up and swung round in a violent U-turn he glanced at Tracy Walsh and Ruth Blantyre.

For once, Detective Constable Beech didn't know which was the worst end of the deal.

Thane used the Millside car's radio for several messages as they streaked across town towards the old Sapphire bingo hall. Part of the result was waiting for him as they slowed and stopped in a side-street about a quarter of a mile from their destination. Two patrol vans were drawn up with their lights out and a mixed squad of uniformed and plain-clothes men aboard.

A bulky figure emerged from one of the patrol vans and stood with his hands in his raincoat pockets till Thane reached him. Chief Superintendent Ilford made

179

it clear he had no intention of being left out of the next stage.

'So far, you're at least half-right,' he said gruffly and without preliminaries. 'We've placed a man on top of another building that practically overlooks this damned hall and he's seen lights moving inside. If you're sure about the rest we go straight in.'

'Into what, sir?' asked Thane. 'We should find out first.'

Ilford frowned and rubbed his chin unhappily.

'If the Burrell stuff is in there – well, maybe you're right,' he conceded reluctantly. 'You and Moss?'

Thane nodded.

'We'll be in position.' Ilford seemed about to add something, then changed his mind. Instead, he brought one hand from his pocket. 'Better take this with you.'

The gun was a Webley .38 revolver. Automatically, Thane checked it was loaded then stowed it in his waist band.

'Don't leave things too long,' said Ilford curtly.

Turning on his heel, he went back to the patrol van.

At night and from a distance the Sapphire bingo hall showed no sign of the fire which had ravaged through it. But at closer range the illusion was dispelled. Outside paintwork blistered and blackened, windows boarded up, it was a dead misery of brickwork with the moonlight showing gaps in the long, peaked roof.

Leaving the Millside car to wait with the patrol vans, Thane and Moss walked the rest of the distance then took stock from a darkened shop doorway. The main entrance to the one-time cinema was guarded by an iron trellis-work gate, the steps behind it almost buried in accumulated rubbish, and a barrier of corrugated-iron sheeting blocked the gap where doors and pay-box had once been located.

'Round the back?' queried Moss.

Thane nodded. A dark lane ran down one side of the building, still with the notice 'Car Park' hanging drunkenly beside it.

He let his fingers touch the cold metal of the Webley and wondered if he'd have to use the gun. There was a bitter irony in it all. He was the reason Jarrold Walsh was now almost certainly somewhere inside that gutted shell. He'd pushed the club owner, tricked and pressured him in the hope something like this would happen.

And now it had, he almost regretted it in the new uncertainty he'd known ever since they'd left Ruth Blantyre.

'Let's get on with it,' muttered Moss impatiently, shivering a little in the light wind. 'Much more of this and I'll get ruddy pneumonia. Or doesn't that matter?'

They moved. The lane was a long, weed-covered tunnel of darkness which emerged into waste ground. At the rear of the bingo hall a high brick wall extended back to encircle its car-park area and they followed it round, moving quietly and keeping close to the shadows.

Suddenly, Thane stopped and grabbed Moss, pulling him back. The car-park entrance was ahead, its large wooden doors closed but with a small service door to one side lying partly open. As they waited, a glowing cigarette stub was tossed out into the night.

Then the service door closed and they heard a lock click shut.

'The natives are restless,' murmured Moss. He glanced above them hopefully and grimaced. 'In case you haven't noticed, there's barbed wire on top of this wall. Do we fly over it?'

'I'm thinking.' Thane looked back the way they'd come. 'Phil, how did you get into a cinema when you were a kid?'

'Me?' Moss sucked his teeth then understood. 'Well, none of us paid. We sneaked in through a lavatory window and hoped we'd land in the men's room.'

They went back into the lane and found what they wanted, a small frosted glass window located at about head height, one of its panes already broken. Boosting Moss up, Thane supported him against the brickwork while a series of softly muttered curses from above punctuated Moss's attempts to locate the catch.

At last there was a click and a squeak. The window swung open, Moss wriggled through, and in another moment Thane had followed him in.

Narrow and smoke-blackened, the white-tiled lavatory ended at a door which led into a charred, cobwebbed corridor, heavy with shadows but with moonlight reaching it from a hole in the roof above. Further along, a door leading into the main theatre area had been completely burned away.

On the other side were lights and the murmur of voices.

They reached the gap and looked out on a scene which was stranger than any they'd expected.

Part of the rear wall of the fire-ravaged old cinema had collapsed, the stage and screen had vanished and debris littered what had once been the front stalls area. But a tarpaulin screening had been rigged over the broken wall and enough rubble had been cleared to form what amounted to a loading bay.

In it, two large, dark blue furniture vans lay one on either side of an even bigger container truck in the light of a string of battery lanterns. Beside them but

182

over-shadowed by their bulk was a small red Ford coupé, and figures were steadily unloading the vans, carrying packing cases one by one into the maw of the container. Once the container truck was filled – Thane swore under his breath at the simplicity of it all.

Container trucks were commonplace around a seaport city, rumbling to and from the docks or lying in lorry parks waiting for shipping schedules. One more container truck would never be noticed until the time came when it was safe to send its treasure-house contents on another stage towards their final destination.

'Colin. Over there.' His voice a hoarse whisper, Moss nudged and pointed towards their left. 'Full house.'

Four men stood beside one of the vans, watching the other figures at work. The nearest was Don Blantyre, who was lighting a cigarette a few feet away from the rest of the group . . . Jarrold Walsh and his son and a grinning Ziggy Fraser.

'That's it,' murmured Moss happily and eased back. 'Let's leave the rough stuff to Buddha and his heavyweights.'

Feeling the same way, Thane started to back from the doorway. But he stopped short as the three men began a sudden, loud-voiced argument – an argument which came to an abrupt end as Ziggy Fraser side-stepped a wildly swung blow from Jarrold Walsh and, still grinning, moved in again as Frank Walsh grabbed his father and held him back.

Ziggy Fraser's right hand came up and the barrel of an automatic pistol glinted briefly in the lantern light before he brought it in a chopping, sideways blow which took Jarrold Walsh across the temple. The club owner crumpled and would have fallen if his son hadn't kept his grip on him for a moment longer.

The men around the trucks had stopped work,

staring. Fraser swung round, snarled an order, and as the packing cases began moving again Jarrold Walsh staggered a few steps towards a mound of rubble and leaned against it, clutching his head.

Fraser and Frank Walsh began a bitter, low-voiced argument, Don Blantyre a worried onlooker.

'I'd say I guessed wrong,' said Phil Moss grimly from their cover by the doorway. 'But we could still use Buddha.'

'If we could get him in fast enough,' said Thane tautly. One of the vans had been emptied and the half-dozen men loading the container truck were now all working on the second van. 'If there's only one man at the car park gate . . .'

'He'd be easy,' murmured Moss. 'But we'd have to get past that bunch.' Thin face thoughtful, he shook his head. 'There's not a hope.'

'I'll keep them occupied,' said Thane softly. 'You just get that gate opened.'

'You?' Moss scowled. 'Remember what happened to Francey Lang?'

He stopped. Jarrold Walsh was back on his feet again. The club owner took a few wavering steps towards his son, but Ziggy Fraser's gun hand chopped a second time – and, as his father crumpled, Frank Walsh simply turned away.

Moss winced. 'Maybe one of those emergency exits . . .'

'Boarded up,' said Thane with a quick headshake. 'We passed one.' He brought the Webley from his waist band. 'This wouldn't help me. But use it if you've got to, Phil – just get that damned gate open. Now move.'

Moss drew a deep, unhappy breath, took the gun, and nodded. Crouching low, he slipped out of the doorway into the old cinema area, reached the nearest row of scorched, twisted seats, and crawled along behind them. As his thin figure vanished from sight, Thane put his hands in his pockets and stepped into the open.

He had walked halfway towards the vehicles before one of the neds in the loading gang spotted him. The man dropped the packing case he was carrying, stood open-mouthed for a moment, then yelled and pointed.

Every head swung. Thane came on at the same unhurried pace, feet crunching on rubble and broken glass, his face impassive.

'Hello, Ziggy,' he said calmly as he drew near. 'We've been looking for you.'

Muttering, the men from the trucks bunched into a group and glanced around nervously. Don Blantyre shrank back, almost hiding behind Frank Walsh who stared white-faced. But Ziggy Fraser's sharp, hawk-like features barely twitched before the pistol in his hand came round to train squarely on Thane's chest.

'Keep clear of him.' The little ned's cunning eyes didn't leave Thane but his next words were to the men behind him. 'Somebody tell Whitey at the gate. Fast.'

'We'll need to get out,' bleated Don Blantyre in a note of high-pitched panic.

'We will,' snarled Fraser. As one of his men scrambled off through the canvas screen he glared at Thane. 'Right, where's the rest of your squad?'

'Waiting around.' Thane looked past him at Jarrold Walsh, who was struggling to his feet again with blood oozing from a gash on his forehead. He switched his gaze to Frank Walsh and grimaced in disgust. 'You're quite the little hero, aren't you?'

'Shut up,' hissed Frank Walsh. Face still white, he edged closer to Fraser. 'Finish him and we'll get out – now. The rest of the stuff doesn't matter.'

'But he does.' Fraser gave him a quick, cunning grin. 'If there's more of his kind around we need him and your old man – they're our tickets out of here. And there's always the outside chance he's on his own.'

'You're right.' Frank Walsh licked his lips. 'Get that container ready to close up, fast. Don, help them.'

Blantyre and a few of the men scrambled to obey. But one, the heavy, dull-faced thug who had been Fraser's personal 'minder' in the brief battle at Fidra Street, shuffled nearer with another gun in his hand.

'See he's clean,' nodded Ziggy Fraser.

Getting round, the thug rammed the muzzle of his automatic into Thane's back and held it there while he quickly checked him over.

'Nothin',' he said curtly, shoving Thane forward.

Thane shrugged as he saw the container's platform swing up, leaving only the doors to be closed.

'Two million pounds' worth – and now it's all fouled up. You should know better, Ziggy. Never go thieving with amateurs.'

Frank Walsh gave a hoarse, forced laugh. 'Amateurs? It all worked out, Thane – or it did, till that old idiot came nosing over here.' He swung round at his father. 'Damn you, you swore you weren't followed!'

'Does it matter now?' The words came in a weary croak from the older man. 'Frank, if you won't do anything else, at least tell him Tracy wasn't a part of this. You've nothing against her . . .' He let the words die away, wiping blood from his face with one hand.

'Tracy?' Frank Walsh looked surprised, then grinned oddly. 'She just gave me the idea, yapping on about that collection lecture. An idea – and a way of getting out from under you, dear father.'

'Frank' – over by the container truck, Don Blantyre

fidgeted impatiently – 'let's move.' He stopped and licked his lips, as the man who'd gone to warn the gate guard came running back.

'Whitey says all clear,' he reported breathlessly.

Fraser's small, sharp, animal-like eyes considered Thane carefully. Then, uncertain about what he saw, he turned to Frank Walsh.

'We can try it like you planned,' he said softly. 'If it works . . .' He glanced significantly from Thane to Jarrold Walsh. 'They're both your worry, friend – not mine.'

'Like it was with Harry Durman?' asked Thane caustically, wondering what Moss was doing and knowing he had to fight to gain every second. 'What kind of an operator kills his top technician before a job?'

'Durman?' Frank Walsh scowled. 'He got too greedy for his own good' – he sneered round at his father – 'even forgot who found out the way he'd milked the great Jarrold Walsh over this bingo club's takings.'

'But he still brought Ziggy to you.' Thane sensed their audience, even Fraser, was momentarily interested. If he could play it along just a little longer, make them partly forget the outside – 'Isn't that how it was?'

Ziggy Fraser grunted. 'We did a deal. But if you're trying to work another one, Thane, forget it.'

Thane glanced round the ruined building and grimaced. 'I wouldn't call it much of an investment.' He saw Don Blantyre chewing his lip, sensed his anxiety, and nodded towards him. 'What's his angle, Frank?'

'Money, like the rest of us.' Frank Walsh let a note of contempt slide into his voice. 'Don plays the tables too much – and keeps losing.'

'So he covered up for you at the Silk Slipper the

night you sneaked out to kill Harry Durman,' said Thane flatly. He reached for his cigarettes, saw Fraser's gun hand tighten, and stopped the motion wryly. 'Never mind – but you killed him, Frank. Then you got round to his apartment and collected the electronic gear. Right?'

Jarrold Walsh was staring at them in mute horror. But the younger man's face showed only a grim amusement.

'Harry was expecting an extra pay-off,' he countered dryly. 'He got it.'

A man by the container truck sniggered nervously.

'Because you were scared, like you are now?' countered Thane softly. 'Scared because when you wouldn't pay he said he'd tell your father – and you're still scared of him, aren't you?'

Eyes blazing, Frank Walsh stepped forward and cuffed him viciously across the mouth. Blood on his lips, Thane forced a grin.

'There's your "partner", Ziggy – he's a scared, pea-green amateur. Who did he get to dress up like a monkey in that mink coat, looking for an alarm that didn't exist?' He saw the answer in Fraser's scowl. 'Do you know where that coat came from? He nicked it from home, like some schoolkid.'

Ziggy Fraser winced, then growled impatiently.

'You talk too much.' The automatic's muzzle came up under Thane's nose. 'Just remember, if there's as much as a wandering beat cop outside, either he backs off or you die.' He glanced round, freezing the grins on some of the other faces. 'Let's move. You call it, Frank.'

'Right.' Frank Walsh thumbed dispassionately towards his father. 'Two of you heave him in the back of the container truck. Don, you'll drive it – I'll take Ziggy and Thane in the car. Everyone else goes by truck, we stay close together, and if there's trouble along the way Ziggy and I handle it.'

Nodding, the men moved to obey. But as Don Blantyre turned towards the truck he stopped short and his mouth fell open.

'Frank . . .' The warning came quivering from his lips and he stared towards the canvas screen.

A thin line of uniformed men, the last of them still moving in, were framed in the gap. Buddha Ilford, a grim, cold-faced figure, stood two paces ahead of the rest on the fringe of the battery lanterns' light. His hands were still deep in the pockets of his raincoat as he took another step forward.

'Draw batons.' The old-style command came like a low growl from the C.I.D. chief. 'You men, all of you – stay as you are.'

For a moment even Ziggy Fraser stood frozen, his eyes on the line of uniformed and plain-clothes men moving silently towards them, spreading out as they came. Then, swallowing a curse, he seemed to remember the gun in his hand and came to life again, swinging its muzzle back towards Thane.

Almost from nowhere, Jarrold Walsh somehow threw himself across the gap between them. Grappling Fraser, his height and bulk sent them crashing down together and the gun blasted harmlessly as they fell.

But the sound broke the spell for the rest. Men scattered as the line of police began rushing in like a wave. Only Fraser's bodyguard hesitated, his stolid face bewildered, then he brought up his gun as a tall sergeant charged straight towards him.

Thane got there first. Grabbing the ned's gun-arm with both hands, he jerked the weapon up towards the roof and simultaneously smashed his knee into the man's stomach. A second later the sergeant's baton finished the job, sending the ned folding to the ground.

'Thanks, sir.' The sergeant grinned his appreciation – then gave a curse of warning which ended in an exclamation of startled pain as another shot rang out, from behind, and the bullet took him in the shoulder.

Up on one knee beside a motionless Jarrold Walsh, Ziggy Fraser aimed again. But a different, heavier calibre weapon barked first.

A red hole blossomed between Fraser's eyes. His whole body seemed to convulse, the gun in his hand triggered in the same final spasm in a shot which spanged off the side of the container van, and he was already dead as he crumpled across Jarrold Walsh.

The Webley in his grasp still smoking, Phil Moss came over and looked down. Jarrold Walsh was starting to stir, moaning in the silence.

The silence . . . Thane looked round.

It was over. Ilford's men were herding their captives in a tight group against one wall, two of them dragging a last straggler past the mocking, yawning doors of the container van.

He counted heads then paused. Don Blantyre was there. But Frank Walsh – spinning round, he scanned the shadows.

'Thane.' Buddha Ilford's voice made him turn again. The C.I.D. chief was standing on the container's platform, an odd twist to his usually taciturn mouth. 'Up here.'

'But . . .'

'Up here,' repeated Ilford firmly.

He went over, climbed aboard, then understood.

Frank Walsh hadn't run away. Like a frightened child in terror of what lay ahead, he crouched in a corner among the Burrell crates with sheer despair in

190

his quivering attitude. Lying beside him, like some discarded furry toy, was a brown mink coat.

'Walsh' – Thane spoke his name sharply – 'come out.'

The dark head turned slowly and apprehensively. There were tears in the man's eyes and his mouth twitched as he looked around the carefully stacked treasures which he'd come so close to winning.

'No.' It came like a mumble and his head began shaking. 'No . . . no.'

Then what had been a mumble became a long, hideous wail of sickening misery and he burrowed deeper into his corner.

'Leave him,' said Buddha Ilford grimly. 'Someone else can sweep him up.'

They climbed down from the container truck and went over to where Phil Moss was standing. Jarrold Walsh was being helped to his feet by a uniformed man, but Moss was still looking down at Ziggy Fraser's body, the Webley in his hand.

'I'll take it,' said Ilford.

Nodding, Moss handed him the gun.

'Right.' Ilford tucked it away then nodded towards the club owner. 'He's the one I feel sorry for, I suppose. Still, he's got the girl – and the Blantyre woman.'

'He'll need them,' muttered Moss.

'No doubt. Maybe they'll try and prove the son insane.' Ilford gave a brief, mirthless grunt at the thought, then considered Ziggy Fraser's body for a moment without emotion. 'Don't let this one worry you, Moss. Or you, Thane – not now.'

'Sir?' Thane caught an underlying bitterness in the C.I.D. chief's voice.

Ilford shrugged. 'I heard before we moved in – Francey Lang is dead. Something about a haemorrhage that took them by surprise.'

Thane thought of Francey's wife, of the way the community involvement sergeant had grinned and talked when he'd seen him last. He looked down at the man at their feet.

'And this makes a difference?' he asked quietly.

'It does to me – when I'm going to see Francey's wife,' said Chief Superintendent William Ilford wearily. 'I'm Old Testament material.'

He turned and walked away.